THE LIVES OF GREAT ARTISTS

THE LIFE AND ART OF VINCENT VAN GOGH

THE LIVES OF GREAT ARTISTS

THE LIFE AND ART OF VINCENT VAN GOGH

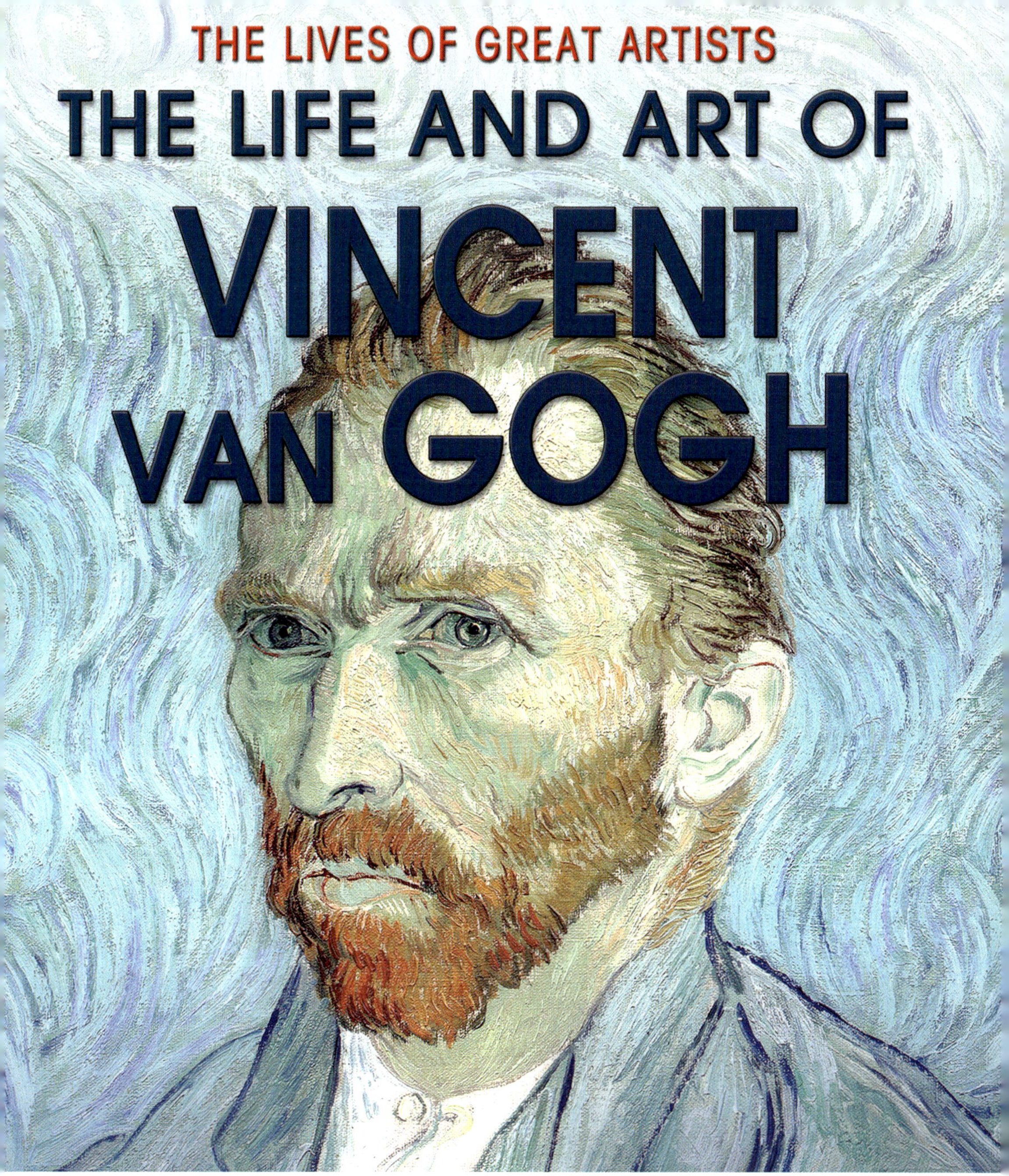

GEORGE RODDAM

ROSEN PUBLISHING®
New York

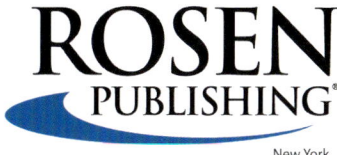

This edition published in 2017 by
The Rosen Publishing Group, Inc.
29 East 21st Street
New York, NY 10010

Additional end matter copyright © 2017 by The Rosen Publishing Group, Inc.

All rights reserved. No part of this book may be reproduced in any form without permission in writing from the publisher, except by a reviewer.

Library of Congress Cataloging-in-Publication Data

Names: Roddam, George, author. | Harasymowicz, Slawa, illustrator.

Title: The life and art of Vincent van Gogh / George Roddam.

Description: New York : Rosen Publishing, 2017. | Series: The lives of great artists | Includes bibliographical references and index.

Identifiers: LCCN 2016039165 | ISBN 9781499465839 (library bound)

Subjects: LCSH: Gogh, Vincent van, 1853-1890—Juvenile literature. | Artists—Netherlands—Biography—Juvenile literature.

Classification: LCC N6953.G3 R63 2016 | DDC 759.9492—dc23

LC record available at https://lccn.loc.gov/2016039165

Manufactured in the United States of America

© Text 2015 George Roddam. George Roddam has asserted his right, under the Copyright, Designs, and Patent Act 1988, to be identified as the Author of this Work.
© Illustrations 2015 Sława Harasymowicz
Series editor: Catherine Ingram

This book was produced and published in 2015 by Laurence King Publishing Ltd., London.

About the Author
George Roddam has taught art history at universities in the United Kingdom and the United States. His research focuses primarily on European Modernisms and he has published numerous articles on the subject. He lives in southeast England with his wife and two sons.

About the Illustrator
Sława Harasymowicz is a Polish artist based in London. Her projects include a solo exhibition at the Freud Museum, London, following the 2012 publication of The Wolf Man (a graphic novel of Sigmund Freud's most famous case), and a solo exhibition at the Ethnographic Museum, Krakow (2014). She has won the Arts Foundation Fellowship (2008) and Victoria and Albert Museum Illustration Award (2009).

Photo credits: All illustrations by Sława Harasymowicz.
6 White Images/Scala, Florence; 8 akg-images; 19 Walsall Art Gallery / Bridgeman Images; 22–23 De Agostini Picture Library/Scala, Florence; 29 akg-images; 33 Photo Scala, Florence / BPK, Bildagentur für Kunst, Kultur und Geschichte, Berlin; 36 Photo Fine Art Images / Heritage Images / Scala, Florence; 38 Private Collection / Giraudon / Bridgeman Images; 39 © Artothek; 44 The Art Archive / Museum of Fine Arts, Boston / Superstock; 55 Photo Fine Art Images / Heritage Images / Scala, Florence; 56 © Painting / Alamy; 57 The Art Archive / Museum of Fine Arts, Boston / De Agostini Picture Library; 59 Photo Scala, Florence/ BPK, Bildagentur für Kunst, Kultur und Geschichte, Berlin; 60 © Samuel Courtauld Trust, The Courtauld Gallery, London / Bridgeman Images; 65 Philadelphia Museum of Art, Pennsylvania, PA, USA / The Henry P. McIlhenny Collection in memory of Frances P. McIlhenny, 1986 / Bridgeman Images; 68–69 Digital image, The Museum of Modern Art, New York/Scala, Florence; 73 Private Collection / Photo © Christie's Images / Bridgeman Images; 74 Photo Scala, Florence; 77 Van Gogh Museum, Amsterdam, The Netherlands / Bridgeman Images; 81 Fogg Art Museum, Harvard University Art Museums / Bequest from the Collection of Maurice Wertheim, Class 1906 / Bridgeman Images.

Contents

A Provincial Dutch Childhood	8
Marked By Tragedy	8
The Suffering of Others	11
Life in London	11
A Religious Calling	11
Miners' Wives Carrying Sacks	14
The Solace of Art	16
Strained Familial Relations	16
Doomed Love	17
Sorrow	18
Van Gogh's Letters	21
The Potato Eaters	24
The Eyes of the Artist	28
Impressionism	31
Memories of Home	31
The Allure of Japan	32
Cormon's Studio	34
Post-Impressionism	34
Van Gogh's Madness?	37
Café Table with Absinthe	37
Bridges Across the Seine at Asnières	38
The Yellow House	42
The Bedroom	42
A Rare Friend	45
Postman Joseph Roulin	45
Brotherly Love	47
A Troubled Mind	47
The Night Café	51
The Harvest	54
Sower with Setting Sun	57
Gauguin's Visit	58
Sunflowers	58
Crisis	61
The Asylum at St-Rémy	62
Moments of Lucidity	63
Rain	64
The Starry Night	66
Back to the North	70
Auvers-sur-Oise	71
Portrait of Dr Gachet	72
The Church in Auvers-sur-Oise	75
A Final Crisis	76
Wheat Field with Crows	76
The End	79
Life After Death	80
Self-Portrait Dedicated to Paul Gauguin	80
Glossary	82
For More Information	83
For Further Reading	85
Bibliography	86
Index	87

Vincent van Gogh used art to express his intensely emotional response to the world around him. Alternately enraptured by the beauty of nature and tormented by the sorrows of human existence, he produced in his tragically short life some of the most emotionally expressive paintings ever seen. In a self-portrait painted a year or so before his death he shows himself as a tormented soul, his piercingly blue eyes staring out at us in anguish. His brow is furrowed and he seems barely to see us, instead remaining lost in his own thoughts, while around him the agitated blue background writhes and twists as though in response to his troubled mental state.

Some of his contemporaries made the mistake of thinking him mad, and it is true that he suffered from periods of mental disturbance; in fact, this portrait was painted during a self-imposed stay in an asylum in the south of France. But it is not the work of a madman. The portrait relies on Van Gogh's knowledge of the innovations of his fellow artists, whose advances he turned to newly expressive uses in his work. In the hundreds of letters that he wrote to his beloved brother Theo he discussed with the utmost lucidity how colour and line would help him to realize the goal he had set himself as an artist: to convey both the ecstasy and the despair of life.

A Provincial Dutch Childhood

Van Gogh was born on March 30, 1853 in the small Dutch village of Groot Zundert, close to the Belgian border. His father Theodorus, whose sober piety would greatly affect Van Gogh's outlook on life, was a Protestant minister in the Dutch Reformed Church. His mother Anna, daughter of a bookbinder, instilled in her son a lifelong love of reading.

There was little in Van Gogh's childhood to suggest the troubled life to come. His parents' marriage was strong and he got on well with his five younger siblings – particularly his sister Willemien and his brother Theo, to whom he would always remain close. His father's income was modest, and life in the family home was far from luxurious, but his parents were able to give their children good educations, as well as allowing them to develop their talents. Members of the extended family also helped to broaden the children's horizons. Three of Van Gogh's uncles – Hendrik, Vincent, and Cornelis – were involved in the art trade and would provide him and Theo with their entrée into that world.

Marked By Tragedy

Despite the tranquillity of these early years, there were intimations of tragedy. Van Gogh's birth was marked by unhappy memories: he shared his name with an older brother who had died at birth and who had been born exactly one year before him. As part of the family history, perhaps this event haunted his childhood and later life. Van Gogh was a serious child, silent and thoughtful, as early photographs tend to confirm.

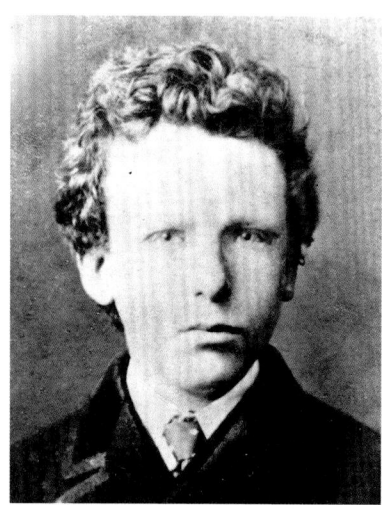

Vincent van Gogh as a pupil, 13 years old. Portrait photo, c. 1866
Van Gogh Museum, Amsterdam (Vincent van Gogh Foundation)

As a child Van Gogh admired his father, but in later life he remembered him as a rigidly principled, distant figure who was insensitive to his children's emotions. As he said in a letter to Theo on December 18, 1883, "there's something very narrow-minded, or rather icy cold, about Pa." When he visited his family he enjoyed conversations with Willemien but found it hard to communicate with his parents.

The Suffering of Others

After his day's work in the gallery, Van Gogh would spend his evenings studying the Bible. His religious faith was very strong at this time, inspired partly by his upbringing within the Dutch Reformed Church, but increasingly driven by a deeply felt and instinctive sympathy for the poor and the wretched. He was also drawn to the work of the English novelists Charles Dickens and George Eliot, admiring their accounts of needy, ill-fated lives. The concern for those less fortunate than himself would stay with Van Gogh for the rest of his life.

Life in London

Van Gogh did well at Goupil and in 1873, at the age of twenty, he was transferred to the firm's London branch. For a time he was happy there, and in his spare time he enjoyed sketching the sights around his lodgings in Brixton. Soon, however, an unrequited passion for his landlady's daughter, Eugénie Loyer, unhinged him. Thrown into despair after her rejection, London became a nightmare for Van Gogh and he isolated himself. This was the first instance of what would become a recurring pattern in his life: periods of relative happiness brought abruptly to a close by an emotional crisis that plunged him into despair and led him to shut himself off from those closest to him.

A Religious Calling

As a result of his unhappiness, in 1874 Uncle Cent had Van Gogh transferred to Paris. However, growing more and more fervently pious, he came to resent the overly commercial aspects of Goupil's art business. His dissatisfaction became apparent to the firm's customers, and in 1876 he was dismissed. He returned to his parents' house in Etten, where he engaged his father in such heated discussions of Christian doctrine that Theodorus became alarmed and sought to persuade his son to pursue other careers. But after short stints as a school teacher back in London and as a book-seller in Dordrecht, Van Gogh moved to Amsterdam in 1877, where he lodged with his Uncle Jan, and began studying for the state examinations in theology. Despite his father's misgivings, the family continued to support him. The dry study of Latin and Greek, however, left Van Gogh cold. He felt they had nothing to do with the teachings about compassion and love for one's fellow man that he found in the Bible. Disastrously underprepared, he failed the exams badly.

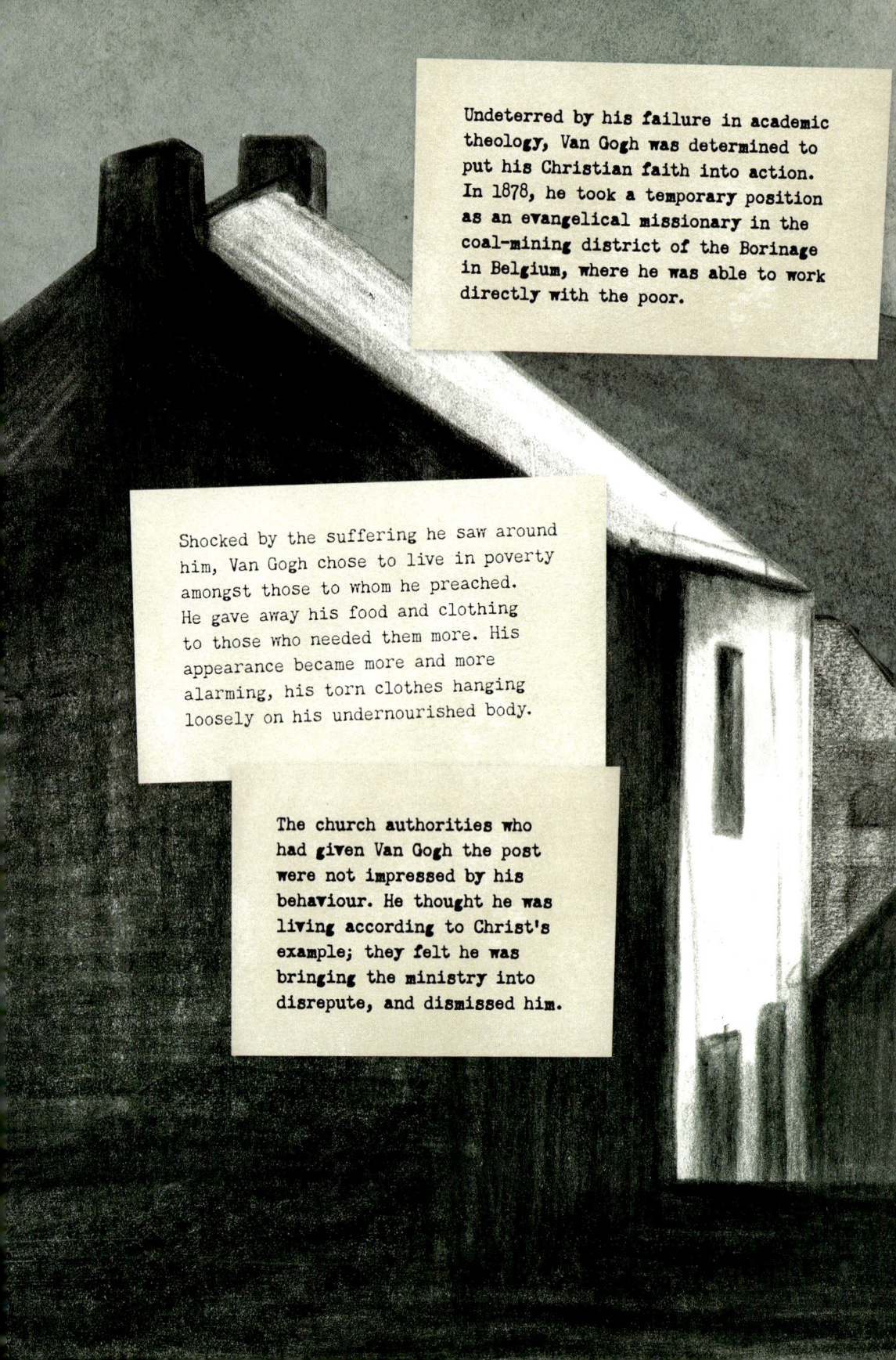

Undeterred by his failure in academic theology, Van Gogh was determined to put his Christian faith into action. In 1878, he took a temporary position as an evangelical missionary in the coal-mining district of the Borinage in Belgium, where he was able to work directly with the poor.

Shocked by the suffering he saw around him, Van Gogh chose to live in poverty amongst those to whom he preached. He gave away his food and clothing to those who needed them more. His appearance became more and more alarming, his torn clothes hanging loosely on his undernourished body.

The church authorities who had given Van Gogh the post were not impressed by his behaviour. He thought he was living according to Christ's example; they felt he was bringing the ministry into disrepute, and dismissed him.

Miners' Wives Carrying Sacks

Memories of the suffering he witnessed in the Borinage stayed with Van Gogh long after he left the area. Over the next two years he expressed his sympathy for the workers in a series of paintings and drawings of miners' wives carrying heavy coal sacks across a bleak landscape. In one particularly heartfelt drawing the women are bent double under the weight of their load as though each step forward is a real struggle. The dark image, heavily worked in black ink and pencil, offers a powerful picture of the dirty and polluted countryside in which the miners and their families laboured.

For Van Gogh this was not just a picture of the hard lives of a particular set of workers. By including the small Christian shrine nailed to the tree and the church steeple on the horizon he transformed the image into a broader symbol of human sorrow. Hence the alternate title he gave to the work: *The Bearers of the Burden*. The crucified Christ in the shrine resonates with the life of suffering to which Van Gogh believed these women were condemned. Perhaps, as he looked at their bodies and clothes caked in coal dust, he recalled a verse from the Bible: "By the sweat of your brow you will eat your food until you return to the ground, since from it you were taken; for dust you are and to dust you will return" (Genesis 3:19).

Although he wanted these women to symbolize human life as a whole, Van Gogh was keen to represent their appearance accurately. In a letter to his friend and fellow Dutch artist Anthon van Rappard on October 29, 1882, he described in detail how they carried their burden:

> I've finally discovered, not without difficulty, how the women miners in the Borinage carry their sacks.... The *opening* of the sack is tied shut and hangs *downwards*. The corners at the bottom are tied together and this creates that charming sort of monk's cowl.

Van Gogh would always remain true to this approach, seeking to combine a close examination of the appearance of things with a powerful expression of his feelings about the world.

Miners' Wives Carrying Sacks /
The Bearers of the Burden
Vincent van Gogh, April 1881

Pencil, ink and watercolour on paper
47.5 x 63 cm (18¾ x 24¾ in)
Kröller-Müller Museum, Otterlo

The Solace of Art

After his dismissal from the Borinage mission, Van Gogh turned from religion to his other great passion, art. He wrote to Theo describing his love of the Barbizon School, a group of French painters who devoted themselves to down-to-earth depictions of peasants and the rural landscape. He also professed an overwhelming passion for Jules Breton, an artist known for his idealized images of pious peasants. (In 1879 he walked all the way to Breton's studio in the French village of Courrières, but was too nervous to introduce himself.) Theo realized that his brother's last chance of happiness lay in following his artistic calling, and in 1880 he encouraged him to enrol at the Académie Royale des Beaux-Arts, the official government art school in Brussels. Classes in anatomy, modelling, and perspective helped to refine his drawing style, but Van Gogh was infuriated by the rigid syllabus and the dry precepts of the teachers. He moved instead to The Hague to study with his cousin-in-law Anton Mauve, a leading member of The Hague School (the landscape artists Van Gogh had become so familiar with during his years at Goupil). Mauve taught Van Gogh to use oil and watercolour, but the two fell out over a request to make drawings from plaster casts – a tedious student exercise that reminded Van Gogh of his time at the Brussels Académie. The fight with Mauve was typical of Van Gogh's relations with colleagues: the intensity of his feelings and his readiness to express his thoughts forcefully meant that he often alienated those closest to him.

Strained Familial Relations

Van Gogh's uncles were increasingly irritated by his refusal to pursue what they saw as a respectable career. In their eyes he had failed at Goupil, and when he gave up the chance to follow his father into the safe profession of minister in the Dutch Reformed Church, they washed their hands of him. Theodorus, too, was concerned by what he saw as his son's erratic behaviour – so much so that in 1880 he considered having him committed to an asylum. Even with Theo there were tensions. After an argument in 1879 about Van Gogh's future, the two brothers had barely communicated for a year. But when Van Gogh decided to become an artist their relationship grew close once more, and thereafter Theo would loyally support his brother, despite their frequent quarrels. After Van Gogh argued furiously with their father on Christmas Day 1881, Theo – who had by now followed Van Gogh into the Hague branch of Goupil – became his primary source of financial support.

Doomed Love

Van Gogh was no luckier with women than he was in his other relationships. During a visit to his parents' house in Etten in 1881 he fell in love with his recently widowed cousin, Kee Vos-Stricker. Van Gogh proposed marriage but, in a repeat of Eugénie Loyer's rejection in London, she turned him down. When she subsequently refused to see him, he visited her father and, holding his left hand in the flame of a lamp, pleaded, "Let me see her for as long as I can keep my hand in the flame." As reported in a letter to Theo on May 16, 1882, her father calmly blew out the lamp and sent him away.

Van Gogh's next involvement was with an alcoholic prostitute, Clasina Hoornik ("Sien"). He met her, destitute and pregnant, wandering the streets of The Hague with her young daughter, Maria. Filled with pity, he took her back to his studio.

In July 1882 Sien gave birth to a son, Willem. Van Gogh was not the father, but for a while he was happy to support Sien and her children. He even contemplated marrying her. But by early 1883 she had started drinking again and returned to prostitution. The small apartment they shared became increasingly filthy and uncared for, and their relationship began to sour.

With his sympathy for Sien waning, Van Gogh threw himself into his work, feverishly recording the working-class people of The Hague. The apartment was filled with hundreds of drawings and paintings depicting the hard lives of the people he saw around him.

Sorrow

While living with Sien, Van Gogh used her as the model for his drawing *Sorrow*. In a bleak and unwelcoming landscape a naked woman sits forlornly, her head resting in despair on her crossed arms. Her swelling belly tells us that she is pregnant, while her gaunt body and the unkempt hair that hangs limply down her naked back make clear that she is uncared for, alone in the world at her time of greatest need. This is how Van Gogh had found Sien, but by hiding her face he transforms his depiction of a specific individual into a general image of suffering.

Van Gogh wanted the picture to awaken in the viewer a sympathy for the downtrodden. At the bottom of the sheet he gave the work the English title of *Sorrow*, perhaps intending to send the drawing to London in the hope of finding work with the illustrated press there. He added in French the accusation, "How can there be on this earth a woman alone – abandoned," a line he borrowed from the French historian and moralist Jules Michelet. He also quoted Michelet when he described the drawing to Theo in a letter on April 10, 1882:

> Because it was for you, who understand these things,
> I didn't hesitate to be somewhat melancholy. I wanted to
> say something like "But the heart's emptiness remains,
> That nothing will make full again."

Michelet's lines refer to the sorrow of lost innocence and the ineradicable pain felt by those who have been betrayed in love. This is how Van Gogh saw Sien. Rather than judging women like her, he wanted viewers of the drawing to respond compassionately to their plight.

Although the overall tone of the image is despondent, the spring flowers around Sien's feet and the blossom in the thorny tree suggest the possibility of redemption. For Sien and Van Gogh, however, redemption never arrived. They split acrimoniously in September 1883. Many years later Sien married a sailor in a final despairing attempt to provide a respectable background for her now adult son. But she remained unhappy, and in a tragic echo of Van Gogh's own ending, would herself commit suicide in 1904 by drowning.

Sorrow
Vincent van Gogh, 1882
Pencil, pen and ink on paper
44.5 x 27 cm (17½ x 10⅝ in)
Walsall Art Gallery

Ik voor my vooral als gy hier waart zou
het meer en meer of figuur me concentreeren
Ik zal U even de landschappen op krabbelen
die ik op 't ezel heb.

Ziedaar 't genre van studies die ik zoude verlangen
gy direkt aangreept. Het landschap groot leeren
aankyken in zyn eenvoudige lynen en tegenstellingen
van licht & bruin. 't Bovenste zag ik leder, was
geheel à la Michel. De grond was Superbe
in de natuur. Myn studie is my nog niet zijp genoeg
maar het effekt greep my aan en was wel grijs
licht & bruin zoo als ik het U hier teeken

Van Gogh's Letters

Van Gogh wrote letters compulsively throughout his life, documenting his feelings in many hundreds of missives to his brother Theo and to other family and friends. As he lived alone for much of his life, this correspondence would have helped keep at bay the feelings of isolation and depression by which he would increasingly be afflicted. If there was any delay from his correspondents – and particularly from Theo – he would reprimand them. In addition, he frequently expressed irritation when it came to matters of money. He repeatedly accused Theo of being slow to respond to his requests for money – rather unreasonably, given that Theo himself was not terribly well off, and was the only member of the family still willing to support him. And he often complained that Theo, who had moved to the Paris branch of Goupil in 1879 and was thus well positioned at the heart of the art world, was not trying hard enough to find buyers for his work. These complaints were, for the most part, unjustified, and bear witness once again to Van Gogh's unerring ability to alienate himself from those who cared most deeply for him. But he could also be the most affectionate of correspondents: when Theo experienced his own difficulties Van Gogh would always offer much-appreciated emotional support.

Van Gogh also wrote extensively about art. He described his own pictures to Theo, often adding little sketches to convey their appearance, as in this letter from October 1883. He also discussed the work of other artists, about which he was very well informed. In this letter he compares his work to that of George Michel, a French landscape painter who often depicted agricultural workers. He also tries to persuade Theo to come and join him and take up painting himself. Van Gogh longed for close companions with whom to share his life's work.

The Potato Eaters
Vincent van Gogh, 1885
Oil on canvas
82 x 114 cm (32¼ x 44⅞ in)
Van Gogh Museum, Amsterdam
(Vincent van Gogh Foundation)

The Potato Eaters

After falling out with Sien, Van Gogh returned to live with his parents, who had since moved to the small Dutch village of Nuenen. Although his strained relationship with his father made life uncomfortable, Van Gogh found inspiration in the local peasants. He had previously focused on the miseries of the workers and their poverty, depicting them as exploited beasts of burden. In Nuenen, partly inspired by Barbizon School images of dignified peasants, he became fascinated by the noble honesty of those who worked the land, and sought to convey this.

Theodorus died suddenly in March 1885, and shortly afterwards Van Gogh finished *The Potato Eaters*, a painting based on many studies of the faces and hands of local workers. In a letter to Theo on April 30, 1885, he wrote of his desire to show middle-class art lovers that

> these folk, who are eating their potatoes by the light of their little lamp, have tilled the earth themselves with these hands they are putting in the dish, and so it speaks of manual labour – and that they have thus honestly *earned* their food.

He painted the canvas quite roughly, allowing the atmosphere of a simple peasant house to dominate:

> If a peasant painting smells of bacon, smoke, potato steam – fine – that's not unhealthy – if a stable smells of manure – very well, that's what a stable's for.

By this time Van Gogh had become deeply interested in colour theory, and was keen to apply the lessons he was learning to his own work. He was particularly interested in how his perception of colour changed under low light conditions, telling Theo in the same letter that skin became "something like the colour of a really dusty unpeeled potato." He also noted that the shadows appeared blue, and proposed that the painting be displayed in a gold frame or against a wall with the "deep tone of ripe wheat" in order to set off its rich, dark tones.

Van Gogh had observed how different colours mix while watching weavers at work. He noticed that by interweaving bright colours they could produce a grey that seemed to vibrate rather than looking lifeless. In *The Potato Eaters* he adopted the same practice. The dark areas are composed of different colours mixed together to give a sense of vitality to the picture.

Van Gogh's respect for the nobility of peasant life did not lead him to romanticize it. In contrast to the Barbizon artists and painters like Jules Breton, who tended to underplay the tough realities of rural life, Van Gogh understood that the peasants laboured hard in the fields to bring their meagre supper to the table. He was equally attuned to the demands of the work carried out by the weavers. In his images of them working at their looms they often seem trapped within the mechanism, suggesting the inescapability of poverty.

In the late nineteenth century, Paris was the capital of the art world, and in Theo's gallery Van Gogh saw the vivid colours and spontaneous brushstrokes of the Impressionists for the first time. Their goal was to record exactly the impression left on the retina by the colours of the world.

After Theodorus's death, and a quarrel with his sister Anna, Van Gogh left Nuenen to study in Antwerp, as Jules Breton had done years before. He ate poorly, though, and drank a great deal of absinthe. Lonely and dispirited, in the spring of 1886 he decided to join Theo in Paris.

In September/October 1886 Van Gogh wrote to his Antwerp friend Horace Livens that, while not yet "one of the club" himself, he admired the work of the Impressionists Monet and Degas. He emulated their use of colour in flower studies painted in oppositions of blue/orange, red/green, and yellow/violet.

The Van Gogh brothers shared a small apartment in the bohemian quarter of Montmartre, an area popular with artists and entertainers. Theo paid the rent, and also provided his brother with money to live on.

The Eyes of the Artist

While in the Netherlands and Belgium, Van Gogh had been concerned with the suffering of the poor. In Paris he became more interested in his own torment. In a sheet of several sketched self-portraits from 1887 he engages in a penetrating self-examination. One of the portraits is rapidly drawn with a few quick strokes of the pencil, but the other is a fully worked up, disturbingly frank image of the artist. We imagine him sitting alone in his studio, peering intently at his reflection in a mirror. The intensity of his gaze is matched by his forceful technique: the pencil has been applied with such vigour that it has partly gouged the surface of the paper. Van Gogh gives particular attention to the eyes, sketching an extra one at the top of the sheet. Two years before, writing to Theo from Antwerp on December 19, 1885, he had declared, "I'd rather paint people's eyes than cathedrals, for there's something in the eyes that isn't in the cathedral ... the soul of a person."

Montmartre: Windmills and Allotments
Vincent van Gogh, 1887
Oil on canvas
45.2 x 81.4 cm (17¼ x 32 in)

Impressionism

Van Gogh was as fascinated by the world around him as he was by his own face. He painted many vibrant views of the area near the Montmartre apartment he shared with Theo. In *Montmartre: Windmills and Allotments* he depicts the small fields that were still to be found in the quarter on the edge of the city, and above them the windmills that stood atop the hill. Van Gogh responds here to the lessons he had learnt from looking at Impressionist works. The brushwork has acquired a sense of immediacy, and the dark tones of *The Potato Eaters* are replaced by bold blues, yellows, and greens, transforming the landscape into a luminous evocation of a brightly sunlit day. The dabs of pure red that dot the foreground capture the intensity with which Van Gogh experienced the colours of the world.

Memories of Home

Van Gogh may have depicted what his eye saw, but here he also carefully selected the viewpoint. One of the windmills on the hill had, by this time, been converted into the infamous nightclub Le Moulin de la Galette, but in this picture Van Gogh gives little attention to this urban side of Montmartre. Instead he concentrates on the agricultural scene in the foreground and the two small figures who work the land. The components of the picture – rural workers and windmills – perhaps reminded him of his homeland. Even as he learnt from the Impressionists that painting could simply record how one saw the world, Van Gogh continued to evoke more deeply felt emotions too, such as a sense of connection to the land.

The Allure of Japan

When Japan was opened up to the West in the 1850s, following centuries of isolation, a widespread fascination with the country and its culture swept through Europe. Van Gogh had been captivated by the strong colours and clean lines of the Japanese woodblock prints that he first discovered in Antwerp, and he continued to collect after his move to Paris. Unlike most of his contemporaries, for whom Japanese objects were merely a passing fashion, Van Gogh felt that European art could reinvigorate itself by learning from the powerful simplicity of these images. He also believed that Japanese culture looked more kindly on artists, imagining a kind of utopia in which they lived in supportive communities, free from the need to find buyers for their work. This was an entirely mistaken view, but it helps to explain Van Gogh's deep attachment to the idea of Japan.

In his copy of Hiroshige's *Plum Estate, Kameido*, Van Gogh follows the original closely, but with important changes. The colour becomes more intense, particularly in the fiery red and saturated yellow of the sky. He also adds a red frame with invented "Japanese" characters that makes the green of the grass appear much more vibrant. Van Gogh was interested in how the use of complementary hues – those found opposite each other on the colour wheel – could make colours seem more intensely vivid. His energetic brushwork also adds to the striking vitality of this image of the simple beauty of nature. When his cousin Mauve had asked him to copy plaster casts he had refused. Here he engages in a more creatively transformative act of copying.

Utagawa Hiroshige (Ando)
Plum Estate, Kameido (Kameido Umeyashiki), No. 30 from *One Hundred Famous Views of Edo*, 11th month of 1857

Woodblock print
Sheet: 36 x 23.5 cm
(14⅛ x 9¼ in)
Brooklyn Museum
Gift of Anna Ferris,
30.1478.30

Japonaiserie: Flowering Plum Tree (after Hiroshige)
Vincent van Gogh, 1887
Oil on canvas
55 x 46 cm (21⅝ x 18⅛ in)
Van Gogh Museum, Amsterdam

Cormon's Studio

When he first arrived in Paris, Van Gogh started attending classes at the studio of Fernand Cormon, hoping to be able to improve his draughtsmanship. Cormon had a favourable reputation among younger artists for his liberal approach to teaching. Although, like Mauve, he still demanded that his students copy plaster casts, he also encouraged them to produce sketches of life on the Paris streets. Van Gogh spent many hours wandering the avenues and alleys around Cormon's studio, jotting down his impressions of the people he saw around him.

Post-Impressionism

Cormon's studio was a gathering place for Paris's avant-garde, and there Van Gogh became acquainted with Émile Bernard and Henri de Toulouse-Lautrec. Later he also got to know Bernard's friend Paul Gauguin. These young artists had initially been inspired by Impressionism, but were now keen to move beyond it; they had come to feel that it was too concerned with merely capturing the appearance of the world. Bernard and Gauguin played with distorting the shapes and colours of their pictures in order to convey their own emotional response to the world. Toulouse-Lautrec was also interested in making his paintings as expressive as possible, focusing on the sordid activities to be found in Montmartre nightclubs and brothels. The work of these young artists, who came to be known as the Post-Impressionists, inspired Van Gogh. He felt he had suddenly stumbled on a kind of fellowship who, like him, believed that art should convey the painter's deeply felt emotions.

Van Gogh was taken by his new friends to the lively nightclubs of Montmartre such as Le Mirliton. There they enjoyed the racy cabaret acts of famous entertainers of the day like Aristide Bruant, who sang about the struggles of the poor and poked fun at the upper classes.

Van Gogh's friendship with Toulouse-Lautrec, a notoriously heavy drinker and regular frequenter of brothels, could not have been further removed from his fervently pious work as a missionary just a few years earlier.

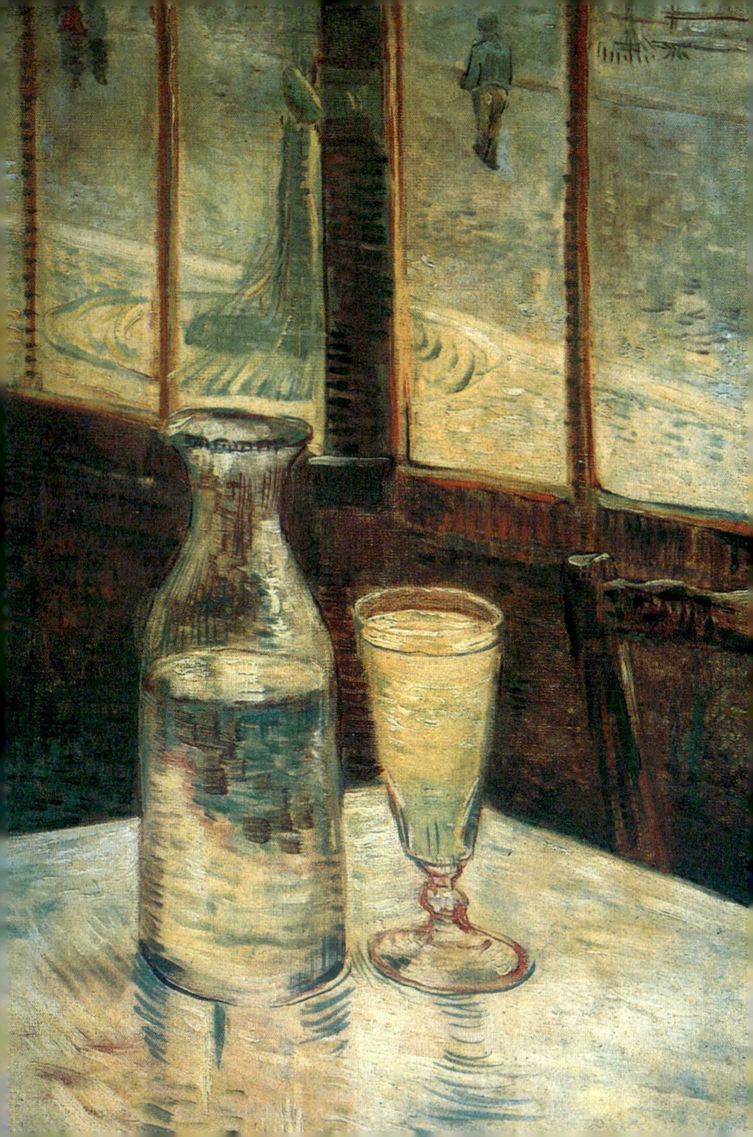

Van Gogh's Madness?

From the time of his unrequited love affair with Eugénie Loyer in London, Van Gogh had displayed signs of mental instability. Prone to fits of melancholy, he could also become wildly angry. What the nature of Van Gogh's illness may have been – and even whether he was really ill – has been debated endlessly. It has been suggested that he may have been epileptic, or that rumoured visits to brothels, which may have started as early as his time in The Hague, might have infected him with syphilis (incurable before the invention of antibiotics), a disease that could lead to delirium. Other suggestions include lead poisoning – the paints he used contained large quantities of this toxic metal – and an addiction to absinthe, the highly alcoholic anise-flavoured drink that many believed impaired the mental faculties of its users.

Café Table with Absinthe

The debate about Van Gogh's mental state will never be resolved. But what can be stated with certainty is that he did not paint as a madman. The popular image of him working in a frenzy could not be further from the truth. In his letters to Theo he repeatedly noted that he only painted at times of mental clarity. *Café Table with Absinthe*, though it depicts the dangerously addictive drink favoured by Van Gogh, is a lucidly composed image. The single glass and the screen of windows separating us from the solitary walker outside have been carefully arranged to convey a sense of loneliness. The painting thus expresses Van Gogh's feelings, but does so by using the tools of art in the most controlled fashion.

Bridges Across the Seine at Asnières

In the spring of 1887 Van Gogh often painted in Asnières, a working-class suburb to the northwest of Montmartre. There he became acquainted with Paul Signac, one of the leading members of a group known as the Neo-Impressionists. Where Post-Impressionists such as Gauguin wanted painting to be more expressive, the Neo-Impressionists believed that breaking colour up into small dots and juxtaposing complementary colours would allow artists to depict light effects with scientific accuracy. Van Gogh, with his interest in colour theory, was excited by Signac's ideas and experimented with the style. However, he found its dry precision unfitted to his excitable temperament.

In *Bridges across the Seine at Asnières* Van Gogh follows the precepts of Neo-Impressionism only in part. The painting makes extensive use of the complementary contrasts favoured by Signac, for example in the juxtaposition of the blue water with the yellow boats, riverbank, and bridge, and in the green strokes added to the water near the red boat under the bridge. But Van Gogh has given his elongated strokes a vibrant energy that is very different to Signac's patient technique. Van Gogh acknowledges the modern aspects of Asnières – in particular the new iron bridge across which the steam train is passing – but he transforms this view of an ordinary Parisian suburb into an image of radiantly sun-filled beauty.

Paul Signac
The Bridge at Asnières, 1888
Oil on canvas
46 x 65 cm (18⅛ x 25⅝ in)
Private Collection

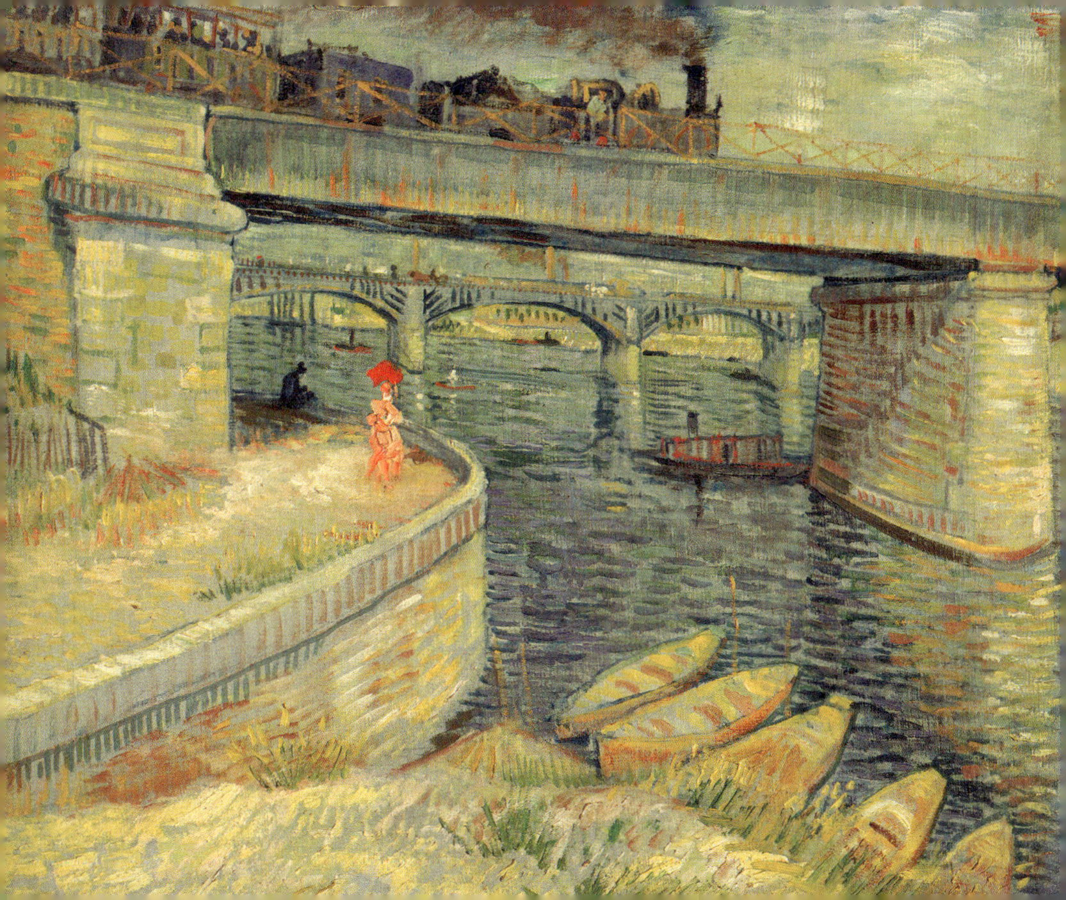

Van Gogh enjoyed working with Signac and others, but found life in Paris hard. In February 1888, exhausted and ill following a desperately cold winter, he moved south to Arles, a small Provence town famed for its Roman ruins and warm climate, where he hoped to recover his strength.

On March 21-22 Van Gogh described Arles's colourful inhabitants to Theo: "the Zouaves [soldiers serving in French North Africa], the brothels, the adorable little Arlésiennes going off to make their first communion, the priest in his surplice who looks like a dangerous rhinoceros, the absinthe drinkers ... seem to me like creatures from another world."

Van Gogh believed that the intense light and rich colours of the south would reinvigorate his painting. He compared Arles to Japan, writing to Bernard on March 18 that the beautiful emerald and rich blue of its landscape resembled Japanese prints.

Van Gogh also hoped to found a utopian artistic commune in Arles, away from the jealous rivalries of the Paris art world. He invited his friends to join him in forming a confraternity where they could paint in peace free from the pressures of the market.

The Yellow House

After two months in a hotel, Van Gogh rented one wing of a house on Place Lamartine, near the centre of Arles. He was drawn to the house in part because of its colour – he associated yellow both with happiness and Japan – and in good spirits, he planned to welcome friends. One of the rooms served as his studio, which was soon littered with used paint-tubes, brushes, and half-finished canvases as he threw himself into creating pictures to decorate his new home. A second room served as his bedroom. The third room he prepared for the guests that he hoped would soon begin to arrive.

The Bedroom

The Bedroom shows Van Gogh's simply furnished room with some of the paintings he created to decorate the Yellow House already hanging on the walls. The image shows fairly accurately the layout of the room, whose far wall was not at right angles to the other walls. But Van Gogh radically simplified the room's appearance. The simple blocks of colour – particularly the soothing harmony of yellow and pale blue – express the sense of tranquillity that, at least for a while, he experienced in this space. He wrote to Theo on October 16, 1888, describing the painting:

> It's simply my bedroom, but the colour has to do the job here, and through its being simplified by giving a grander style to things, to be suggestive here *of rest* or *of sleep* in general. In short, looking at the painting should *rest* the mind, or rather, the imagination.

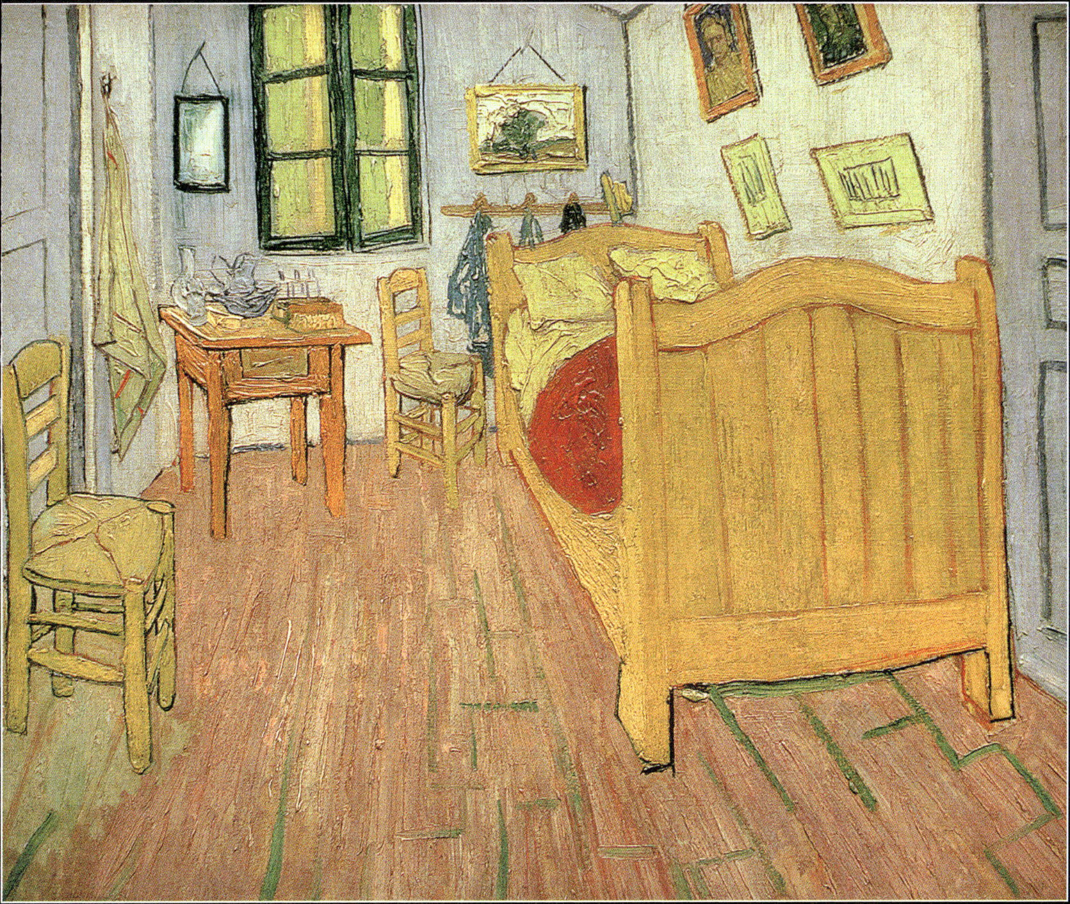

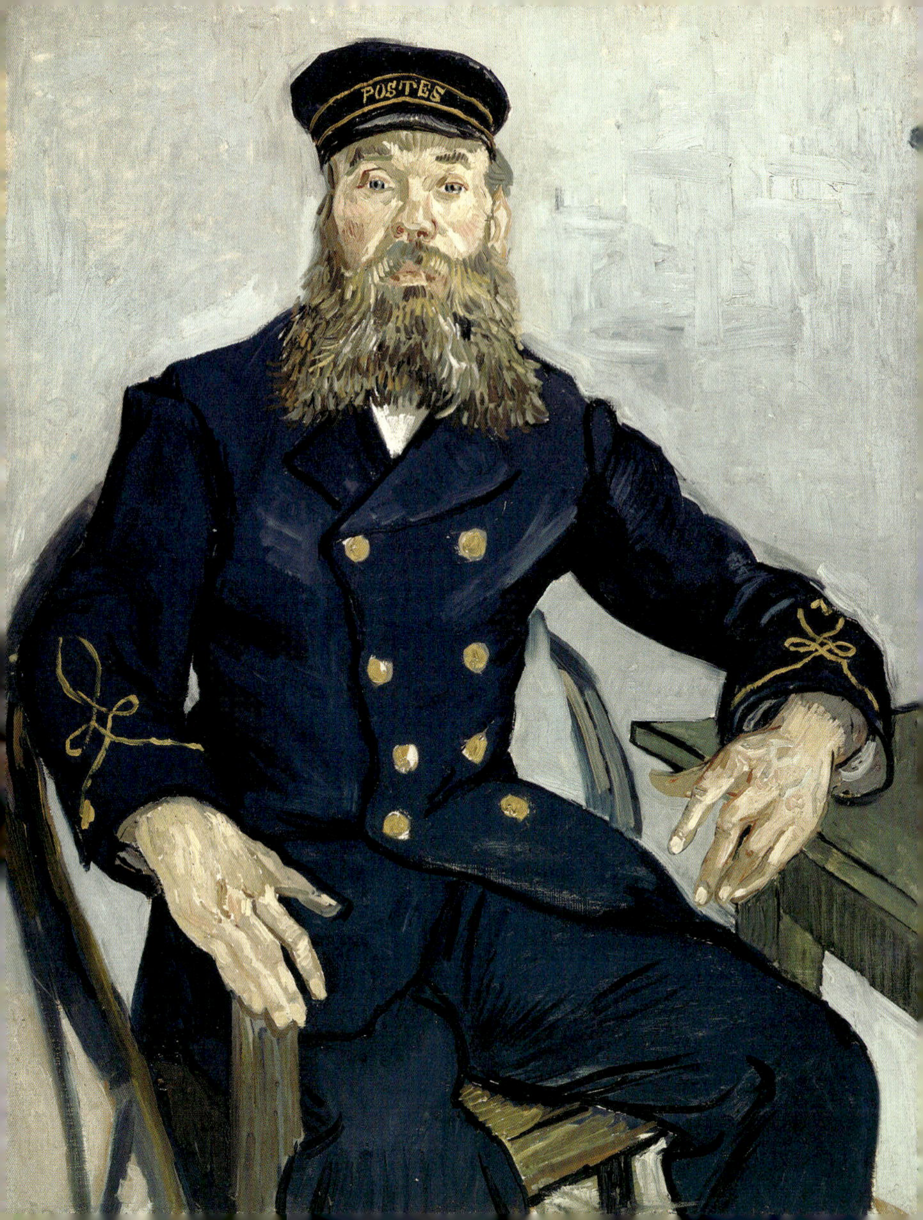
POSTES

A Rare Friend

Although he was delighted by Arles and its picturesque inhabitants, Van Gogh felt himself to be an outsider. Most of the townspeople thought him rather strange: a foreign artist from the north, prone to angry outbursts and fits of melancholy, and who created strange pictures the like of which they had never seen. He did, though, form two or three close friendships. One of these was with the postman Joseph Roulin, with whom he would occasionally drink absinthe at one of the local cafés.

Postman Joseph Roulin

Van Gogh shows his friend in his resplendent blue and yellow uniform. He looks out at us guilelessly, as though waiting patiently for us to converse with him. Van Gogh described him to Theo on July 31 as "a raging republican" who regularly gave vent to his fierce opinions. With his long-standing sympathy for the common man, Van Gogh was drawn to the blunt honesty of Roulin's working-class opinions. To convey his view of this uncomplicated and sincere man, he simplified the colours of the painting and the contours of the clothing. The declaredly unsophisticated technique is the pictorial equivalent of what Van Gogh saw as Roulin's straightforward nature.

Van Gogh was entranced by the Sunday bullfights held in Arles, and a letter to his friend Arnold Koning on May 29-30 describes an occasion when the bull leapt over the barrier and scattered the spectators. The life-and-death struggle between man and animal echoed the intensity he sought in his art.

Apart from occasional drinks with Roulin and one or two others, Van Gogh lived a solitary life in Arles. On July 5 he wrote to Theo that "many days pass without my saying a word to anyone except to order supper." Even in an impassioned bullfight crowd he felt alone.

Brotherly Love

Van Gogh wrote to Theo two or three times a week from Arles, describing everything he was doing and feeling. These letters and the news he received in return were his main form of human contact in Arles and an invaluable record of his time there. He gave extended accounts of what he was working on, and often included sketches to give a better idea of what the new paintings looked like. He was always keen to hear his brother's opinion of his new work, regularly seeking his advice on how best to find an audience for it.

Theo sought in vain to find buyers for Van Gogh's unconventional art, and failed to persuade his boss to display them in the gallery in Paris. He continued regularly to send money to fund his brother's life as an artist, but Theo had money worries of his own and his health was suffering. Most of all, he was increasingly concerned about his brother's state of mind.

A Troubled Mind

Van Gogh's letters reveal that his mental instability was worsening. In one letter he would accuse Theo of neglecting him or of condescending to him, and in the next beg his forgiveness for these unjust accusations. Paralyzed by concerns about his precarious financial situation, he was wracked by guilt over the financial burden he placed on Theo, proposing that everything he painted should be considered his brother's property. Yet he also continued to fret about whether or not his art had any worth at all. On rare occasions he would sound a more positive note; on September 23-24 of the same year he wrote to Theo to say that he hoped his feelings of loneliness would pass with time and that the Yellow House would become a place where he could be at peace, even if alone. But for the most part, the letters reveal a long descent into melancholy, and an increasing sense of alienation from the people around him. The dream that Arles might be his redemption was beginning to fade.

The Night Café
Vincent van Gogh, 1888

Oil on canvas
72.4 x 92.1 cm (28½ x 36¼ in)
Yale University Art Gallery
Bequest of Stephen Carlton Clark, B.A. 1903,
1961.18.34

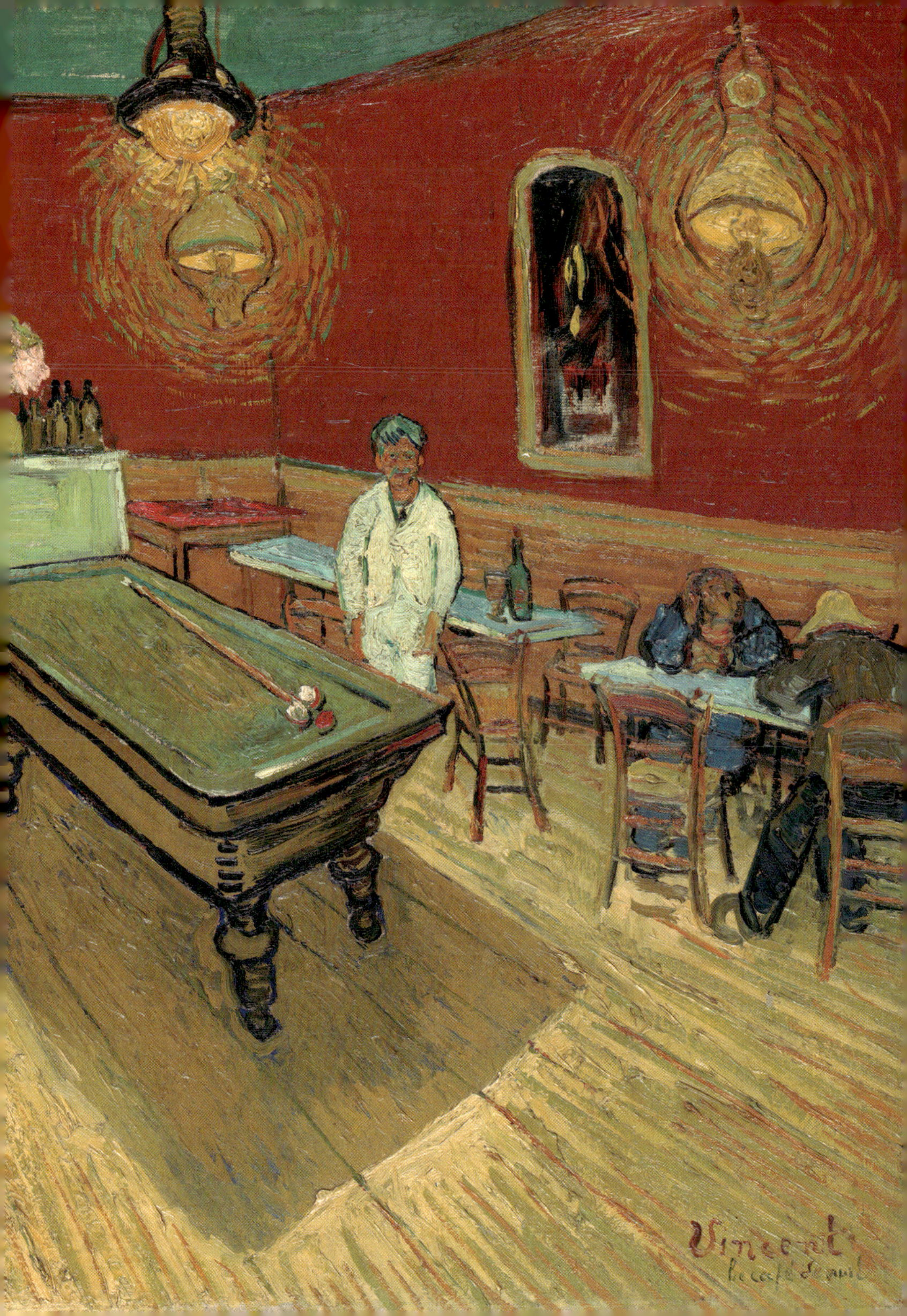
Vincent

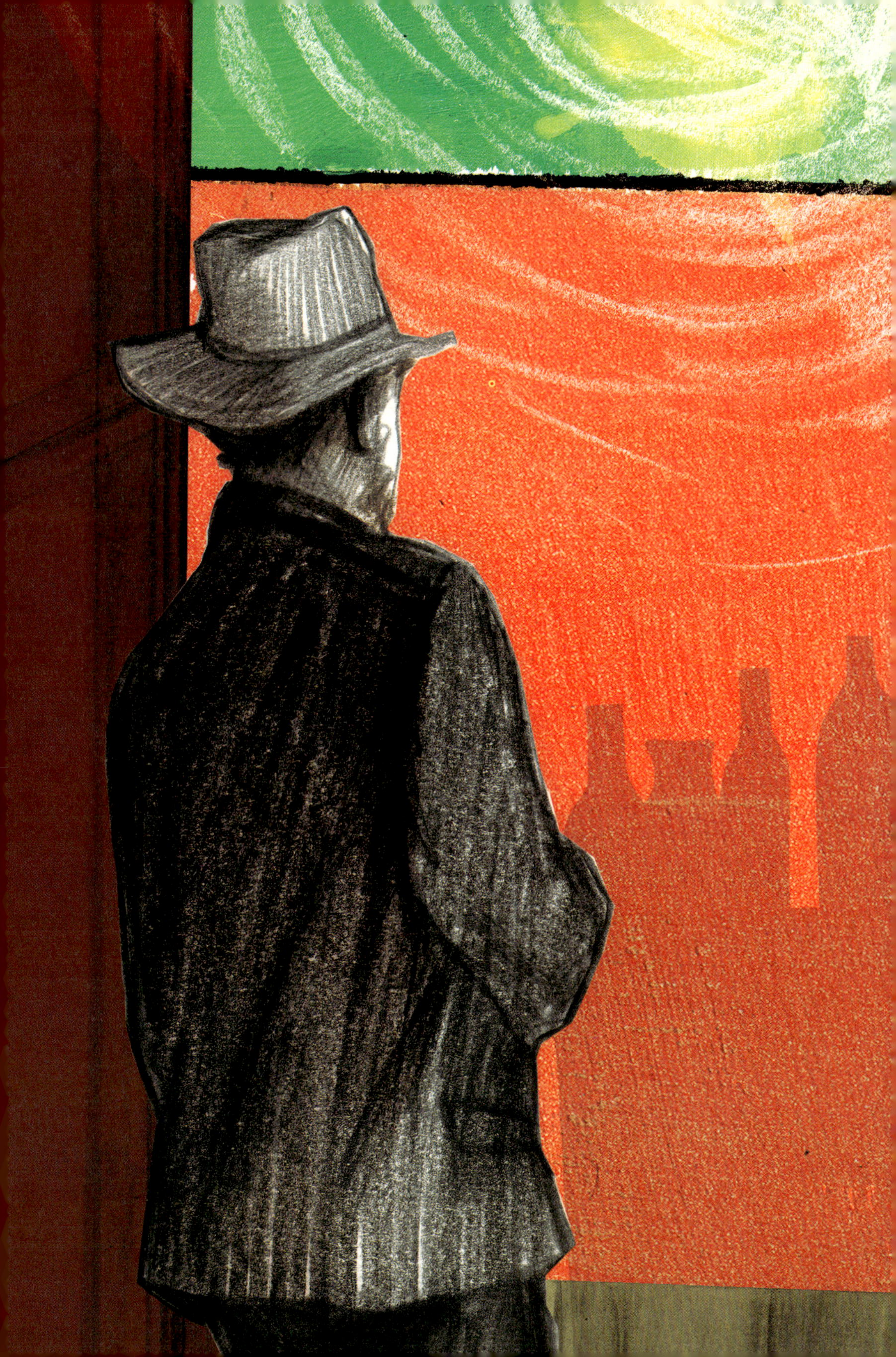

The Night Café

Van Gogh's feelings of alienation are powerfully expressed in his night-time image of the Café de la Gare. Above the café there were rooms to let, and Van Gogh had stayed there when he first arrived in Arles, but after two months he became embroiled in a bitter dispute with the owner, Joseph Ginoux, over how much rent he owed. In a letter to Theo on September 8, 1888 he explains that to get his revenge he had depicted Ginoux's "filthy old place" in one of the ugliest paintings he had ever made. He stayed up for three nights to paint it, sleeping during the day.

We seem to look into the café from the door, as though uncertain whether we should enter this unappealing establishment. Ginoux, hands in the pockets of his white overall, stares out at us unwelcomingly, and the only customers are a few sleeping ruffians and a prostitute and her customer in the corner. The giddily exaggerated perspective creates a sense of vertigo that strengthens our anxiety. The exaggerated shadow under the billiard table adds to the ominous feel of the picture.

In *The Night Café* Van Gogh distorts colour to express his intensely emotional response to the scene. In the same letter to Theo he explained that he "tried to express the terrible human passions with the red and the green," contrary colours drawn from opposite sides of the colour wheel. The jarring contrast of the blood red of the walls and the acidic green of the billiard table and ceiling adds to the painting's oppressively uneasy atmosphere. So too does the queasy intensity of the acid yellow floor and the irradiated haloes of the ceiling lamps.

The painting is perhaps not, however, entirely without sympathy. Van Gogh may have been angry at Ginoux, but he felt sorry for the lonely lives of those who spent the night drinking here. As he expressed to Theo, the painting was "the equivalent, though different, of the potato eaters." However bitter his own experience, Van Gogh never lost his empathy for the hard lives of those around him.

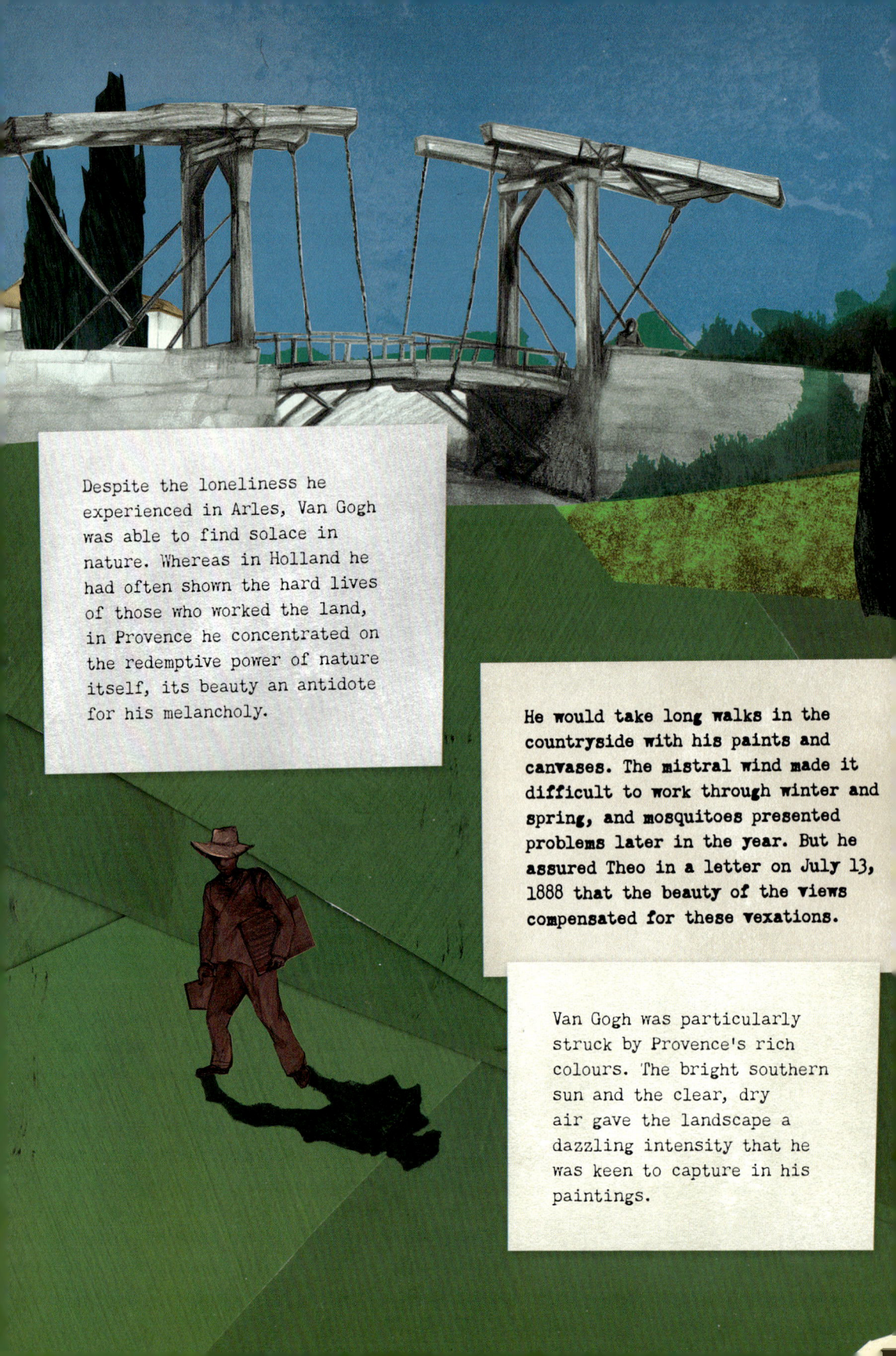

Despite the loneliness he experienced in Arles, Van Gogh was able to find solace in nature. Whereas in Holland he had often shown the hard lives of those who worked the land, in Provence he concentrated on the redemptive power of nature itself, its beauty an antidote for his melancholy.

He would take long walks in the countryside with his paints and canvases. The mistral wind made it difficult to work through winter and spring, and mosquitoes presented problems later in the year. But he assured Theo in a letter on July 13, 1888 that the beauty of the views compensated for these vexations.

Van Gogh was particularly struck by Provence's rich colours. The bright southern sun and the clear, dry air gave the landscape a dazzling intensity that he was keen to capture in his paintings.

Outdoors, Van Gogh was able to hold on to the dream of a life in southern France that was like the Japan of his dreams. As he wrote to Theo on September 21, "here I'll have more and more the existence of a Japanese painter, living close to nature."

The Harvest

One of Van Gogh's favourite hikes took him northeast from Arles across the fertile plain of La Crau to the ruined medieval abbey of Montmajour. He was charmed by the fecundity of the area, writing approvingly to Theo on May 26, 1888 about the quality of the local wine. Writing again on July 13 he explained that he was particularly drawn to the area because its flat expanse reminded him of Holland. As spring gave way to the scorching heat of the Provençal summer he enthused about the vibrant colour combinations that came to dominate the landscape. As he wrote to Theo on June 12-13:

> There's old gold, bronze, copper in everything now, you might say, and that, with the green blue of the sky heated white-hot, produces a delightful colour which is exceedingly harmonious.

The Harvest evokes the radiant light of the south through a careful arrangement of concentrated colour. Van Gogh used his knowledge of colour theory to intensify its effect: the warm, golden hue of the ripening wheat comprises a symphony in yellow whose intensity is increased by being juxtaposed with the complementary blue of the mountains and sky. Where the red and green of *The Night Café* produced a jarring effect, here two colours from opposite sides of the colour wheel are used to generate a very different effect, capturing the radiant beauty of the Provençal landscape.

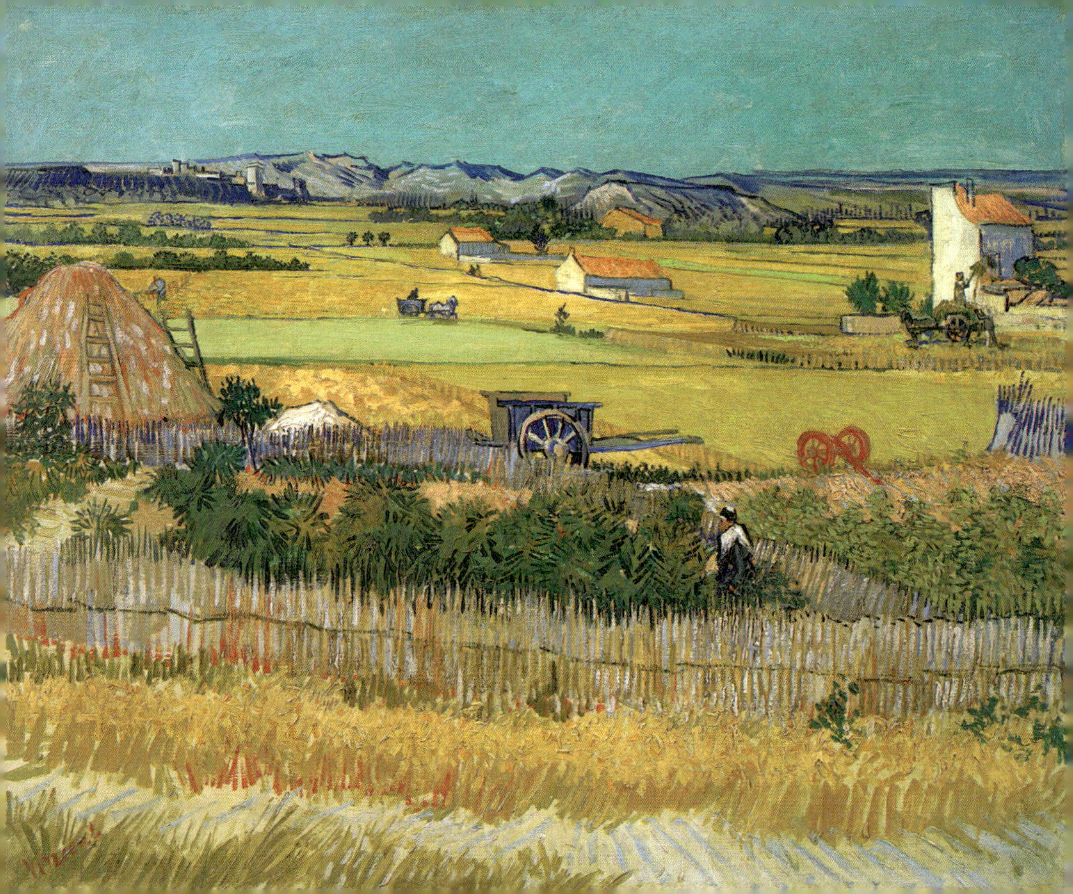

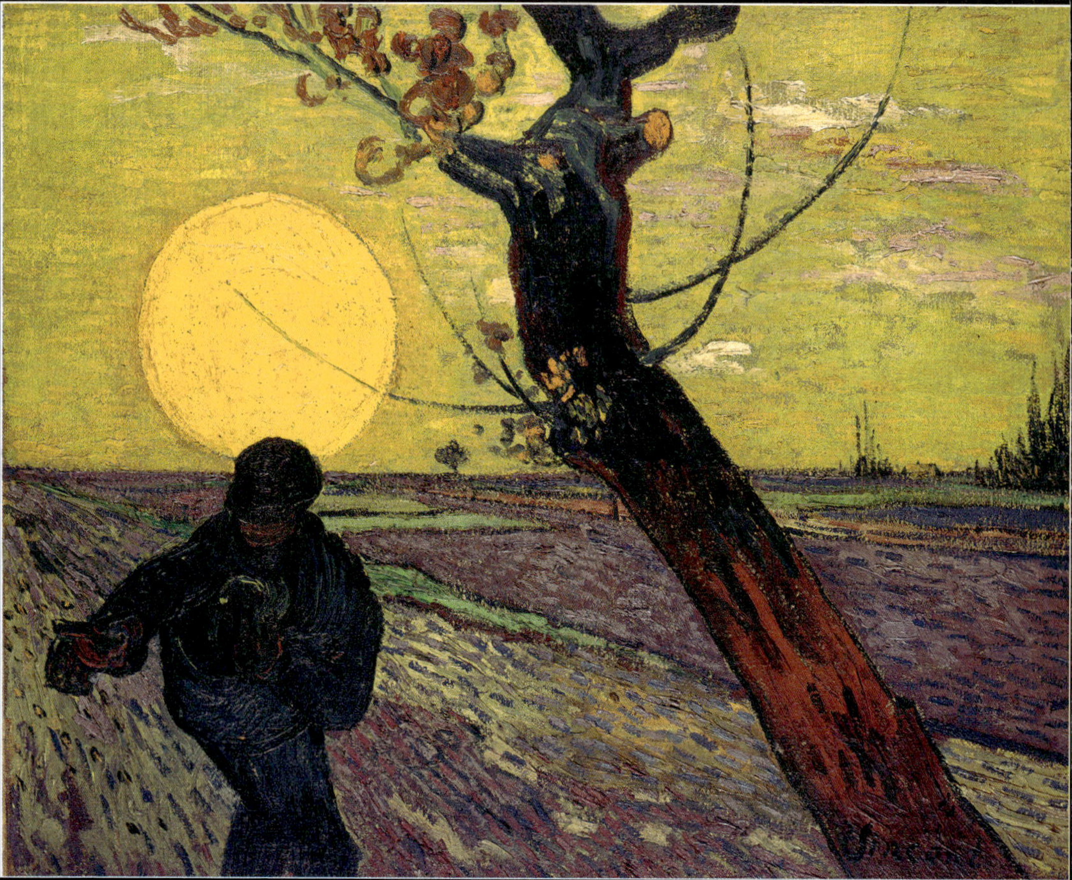

Sower with Setting Sun

Like *The Harvest*, *Sower with Setting Sun* depicts a seasonal rural activity. But where Van Gogh painted *The Harvest* from life, the *Sower* was created in November, when the approaching winter had driven the peasants from the fields. This is an image drawn from the artist's own imagination, based partly on his own memories of watching labourers in the fields and partly on the work of other artists.

The tree trunk that cuts across the image in a dramatic diagonal recalls the powerful graphic lines of Hiroshige's *Plum Estate,* which Van Gogh had copied in Paris. But Van Gogh is most strongly influenced here by Jean-François Millet, one of the leading members of the Barbizon School and best known for idealized images of peasants. He had long been one of Van Gogh's favourites. Van Gogh believed that Millet's works were infused by the Christian virtues of humility and a love of his fellow man; in a letter to Bernard from Arles on June 26, 1888 he declared, "Millet has painted Christ's doctrine."

Here he copies Millet's famous image of a sower but changes it significantly. Where Millet's field is dull brown, Van Gogh uses intense colour for his landscape to express the religious awe with which he looks at nature. The violet shadows in the ploughed field complement the yellow sky, and the red highlights on the tree reverberate with the greens scattered through the fields. Sinking towards the horizon, the immense lemon yellow disc of the sun becomes a halo around the sower's head. Where Van Gogh's earlier *Potato Eaters* had presented a rather somber picture of the hard realities of peasant life, here an ordinary rural scene is transformed into a poetic invocation of God's presence in the cycles of nature. As Van Gogh's mental state worsened, he came more and more to see art and nature as holding forth the possibility of an ecstatic escape from his anguish. Even here, though, his feeling of alienation from the inhabitants of Arles can be sensed. We feel little sense of communion with the sower, who has been transformed into a dark and slightly ominous silhouette.

Jean-François Millet
The Sower, 1850
Oil on canvas
101.6 x 82.6 cm (40 x 32½ in)
Museum of Fine Arts, Boston
Gift of Quincy Adams Shaw through Quincy Adams Shaw, Jr., and Mrs. Marian Shaw Haughton, 17.1485

Gauguin's Visit

In October of 1888, Van Gogh managed to persuade Gauguin to come to stay with him in the Yellow House. In the days before his arrival he excitedly prepared the house, arranging the furniture and hanging paintings on the wall of the guest bedroom, hoping, as he mentioned in a letter to Theo on the 21st of that month, that his dream of founding an artist's colony might be about to come true.

Sunflowers

Van Gogh hoped that Gauguin would appreciate the joyous series of sunflower paintings with which he had decorated the walls of the studio they would share. Yellow, here set off against a blue background, was always seen by Van Gogh as the colour of happiness. He had described the paintings to Theo in a letter on August 21, comparing their simple design and dark contours to the stained-glass windows of a Gothic church. Perhaps he dreamed that he and Gauguin would work together in harmony like the confraternities of nameless craftsmen who had built these medieval structures.

After Gauguin's arrival it seemed for a short while that Van Gogh's dream would become a reality. The two artists found each other's company an inspiration, and they worked side by side, enthusiastically debating their approach to painting.

Sunflowers
Vincent van Gogh, 1888

Oil on canvas
92 x 72 cm (36¼ x 28⅜ in)
Neue Pinakothek, Munich,

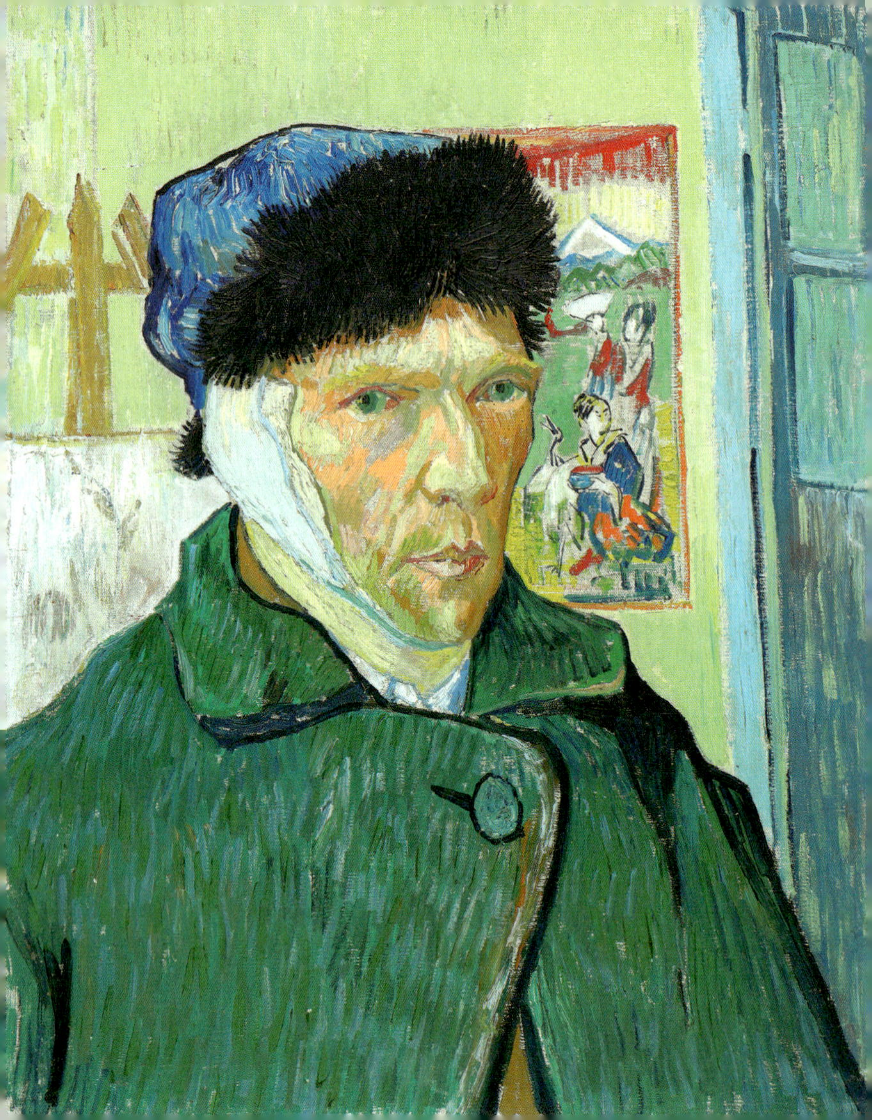

Crisis

Although Van Gogh was delighted to have a companion after six months of solitude, tensions quickly developed between the two men. They argued about whether it was better to paint from life, as Van Gogh tended to do, or from memory, which was Gauguin's preference. When Gauguin made even the smallest criticism of one of his paintings, Van Gogh was thrown into despair, convinced that his friend saw no value at all in his work. He also resented Gauguin's popularity with the local women.

Gauguin, for his part, quickly grew frustrated by Van Gogh's mood swings and, within weeks of arriving, he made plans to return to Paris. Made desperate by the idea that he would once more find himself alone, Van Gogh confronted Gauguin with a cut-throat razor. When Gauguin chose to spend the night in a hotel rather than return to the Yellow House, Van Gogh suffered a mental crisis, severing part of his own ear and almost bleeding to death. He was discovered the next morning and taken to hospital. Gauguin left for Paris without visiting him.

Early in the new year of 1889, Van Gogh, alone again, painted a record of his appearance in the aftermath of the crisis. His wounded ear is bandaged and he is partly lost in his own melancholic thoughts. However, there is also a suggestion of grim determination in his expression. The image speaks of a resolute intention to keep painting despite his difficulties. In the background we see a mostly blank canvas ready to be worked on, alongside one of his beloved Japanese prints.

The Asylum at St-Rémy

Despite his desire to keep working, Van Gogh found it hard to recover his equilibrium. For the first few months of 1889 he shuttled back and forth between the hospital and the Yellow House. In March, during a visit from his old friend Signac, he tried to drink a bottle of turpentine. Disturbed by Van Gogh's odd behaviour, the locals presented a petition to the chief of police demanding that he be taken to an asylum. At first he was confined to the hospital in Arles, then in May he voluntarily committed himself to the asylum at St-Rémy, a small Provençal town 15 miles (24 km) to the northeast. It was Van Gogh's decision to confine himself: the authorities did not think he presented a danger to anyone. He was free to leave whenever he wished, but he would spend the next year there in the hope that he might be cured.

When he arrived at St-Rémy, Van Gogh was optimistic that his doctor, Théophile Peyron, was the right man to help him. But he continued to suffer attacks in the months that followed and grew increasingly despondent. Late in 1889 he again tried to poison himself, this time by eating paint. During his repeated periods of instability he was rarely allowed outside and spent much of his time in the asylum's claustrophobic interior.

Moments of Lucidity

However, during this period Van Gogh also had periods of relative stability. At these times his desire to paint was reawakened, and Theo arranged for him to have two small rooms at the asylum, one serving as his bedroom, the other as his studio where his painting materials could be kept safe. Dr Peyron was happy to allow him to paint under supervision as he believed it might aid his recovery.

Because he had limited access to the world outside the clinic, Van Gogh turned more and more to his memories of other artists' work. He produced a series of paintings reinterpreting the work of Millet. He also created a chilling image based on Gustave Doré's picture of prisoners exercising in a courtyard. In his confinement, Van Gogh identified with the men who are condemned to walk around in an endless circle, hemmed in by the high, dark walls that surround them.

But during periods of prolonged lucidity Van Gogh would be allowed out into the grounds on supervised walks. As at Arles, he was entranced by the vibrant colours of the local landscape. He became particularly fascinated by the olive groves that surrounded the asylum, often sketching the twisted trunks of the ancient trees during his outings. Back in his studio he created vibrant paintings that capture the silver-green colour of their leaves and the clear blue sky of Provence. The energetic brushwork of these images suggests that Van Gogh saw the rugged vitality of these trees as a symbol of hope. Battered by the mistral and the heat of the southern sun, the trees cling on doggedly to life, just as Van Gogh sought to do.

Rain

Van Gogh's windows at the asylum looked out across a field towards the low range of hills known as the Alpilles. During his year in St-Rémy he repeatedly recorded this view, showing how it changed through the seasons. In some paintings we see the young wheat as it first emerges from the ground, while in others the crop has ripened, the golden yellow wheat suffusing the canvas with the warmth of the summer. In other paintings Van Gogh shows the field at the end of the year. He mentioned in a letter to Theo on November 3, that he was working on a "rain effect," making clear that the subject of this picture is the weather as much as the landscape.

Part of Van Gogh's goal was to depict how the scene actually looked. The rain is shown as long streaks of paint, white against the field, black against the sky, in accordance with how the eye sees raindrops as lighter or darker depending on the tone against which they are viewed. But he also distorts the appearance of the world to express his feeling of entrapment: the wall surrounding the field has been made larger than it was in reality, and he has also tilted the wall at the far edge of the field, giving the painting a feeling of disequilibrium that matched his own mental state. We should not, however, think that this is the painting of a madman. As always, Van Gogh only painted when his mind was clear. He also gave careful consideration to how others might perceive his work. In letters to Theo he gave precise accounts of what he was painting and detailed instructions for how he wanted the works to be displayed when he sent them to Paris.

Rain
Vincent van Gogh, 1889
Oil on canvas
73.3 x 92.4 cm (28⅞ x 36⅜ in)
Philadelphia Museum of Art
The Henry P. McIlhenny Collection in memory of
Frances P. McIlhenny, 1986, 1986-26-36

The Starry Night

Another view painted from his asylum window is perhaps Van Gogh's most celebrated painting. *The Starry Night* was inspired by a scene he saw early one morning and which he described to Theo in a letter written sometime between May 31 and June 6, 1889:

> This morning I saw the countryside from my window a long time before sunrise with nothing but the morning star, which looked very big. [Charles-François] Daubigny and [Théodore] Rousseau [Barbizon School artists, like Millet] did that, though, with the expression of all the intimacy and all the great peace and majesty that it has, adding to it a feeling so heartbreaking, so personal. These emotions I do not detest.

With *The Starry Night* Van Gogh sought to put these feelings into his own work. The morning star is joined by other heavenly bodies in a sky animated by a swirling cosmic energy. The cypress trees are equally dynamic, seeming to undulate in sympathy with the rhythms of the heavens. Van Gogh had long dreamed of painting the night sky in this fashion. On April 12, the previous year in Arles he had written to Émile Bernard that

> imagination is a capacity that must be developed, and only that enables us to create a more exalting and consoling nature than what just a glance at reality (which we perceive changing, passing quickly like lightning) allows us to perceive. A starry sky, for example, well – it's a thing that I'd like to try to do.

Although *The Starry Night* was inspired by a real view, it was very much created from the imagination. Van Gogh painted it during the day, relying on his memory of the profound emotions that the morning star had inspired in him. He also relied on other memories. On the horizon are the Alpilles, but the small town, with its prominent church steeple, is an invention that recalls the Dutch villages of his youth. Van Gogh had written nostalgically to Theo between July 17 and 20, 1888 about his earlier life: "Without meaning to ... I quite often think of Holland, and with the double separation of distance and time that has passed, these memories have something heartbreaking about them."

The church that stands at the centre of the village underneath the sheltering canopy of the star-filled heavens also recalls Van Gogh's earlier faith in the ability of religion to bring people together. The warm light that spills out through the windows of the nearby houses suggests families seated around glowing fires inside. This was the life that Van Gogh pined for.

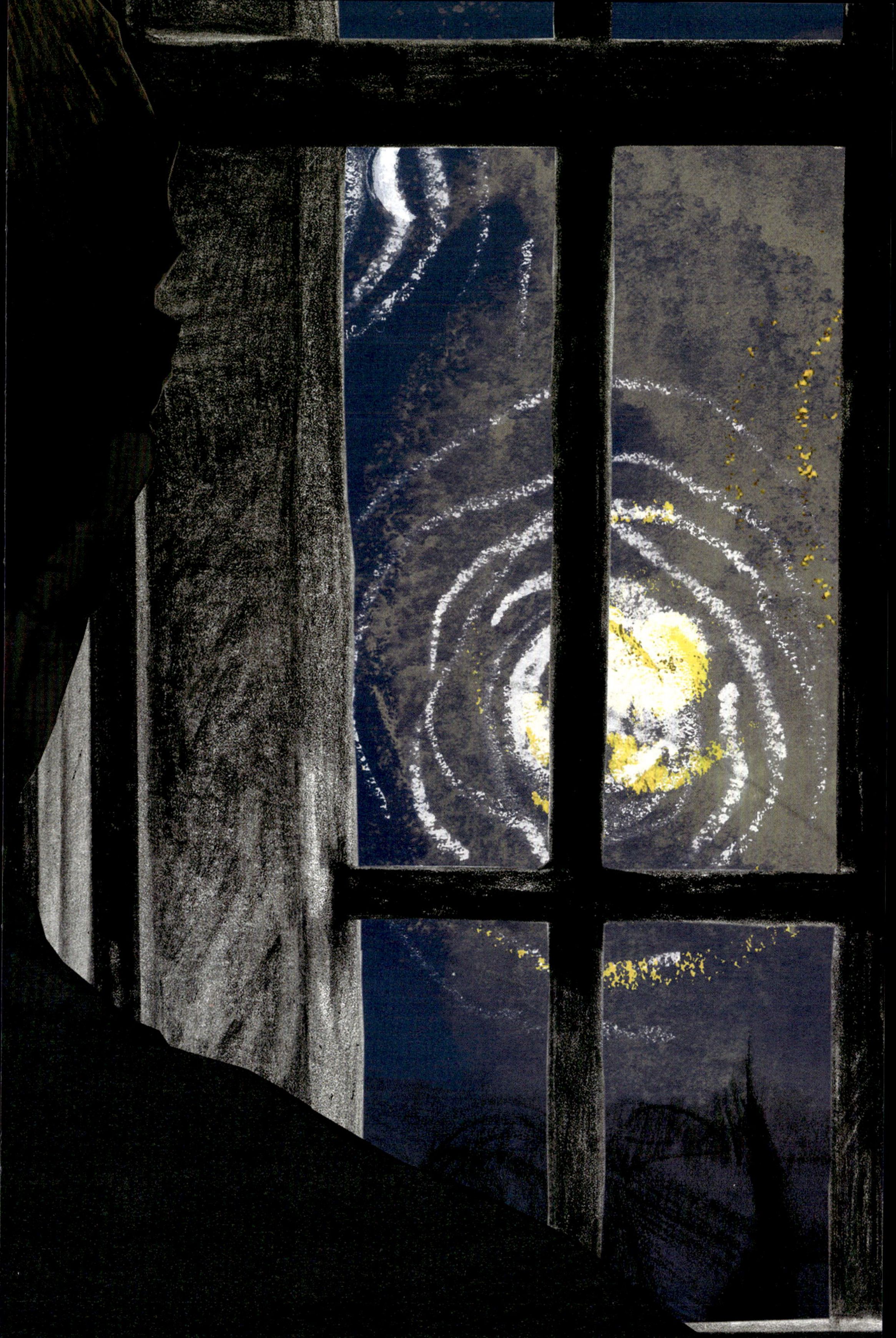

The Starry Night
Vincent van Gogh, 1889

Oil on canvas
73.7 x 92.1 cm (29 x 36¼ in)
Museum of Modern Art, New York
quired through the Lillie P. Bliss Bequest,
472.1941

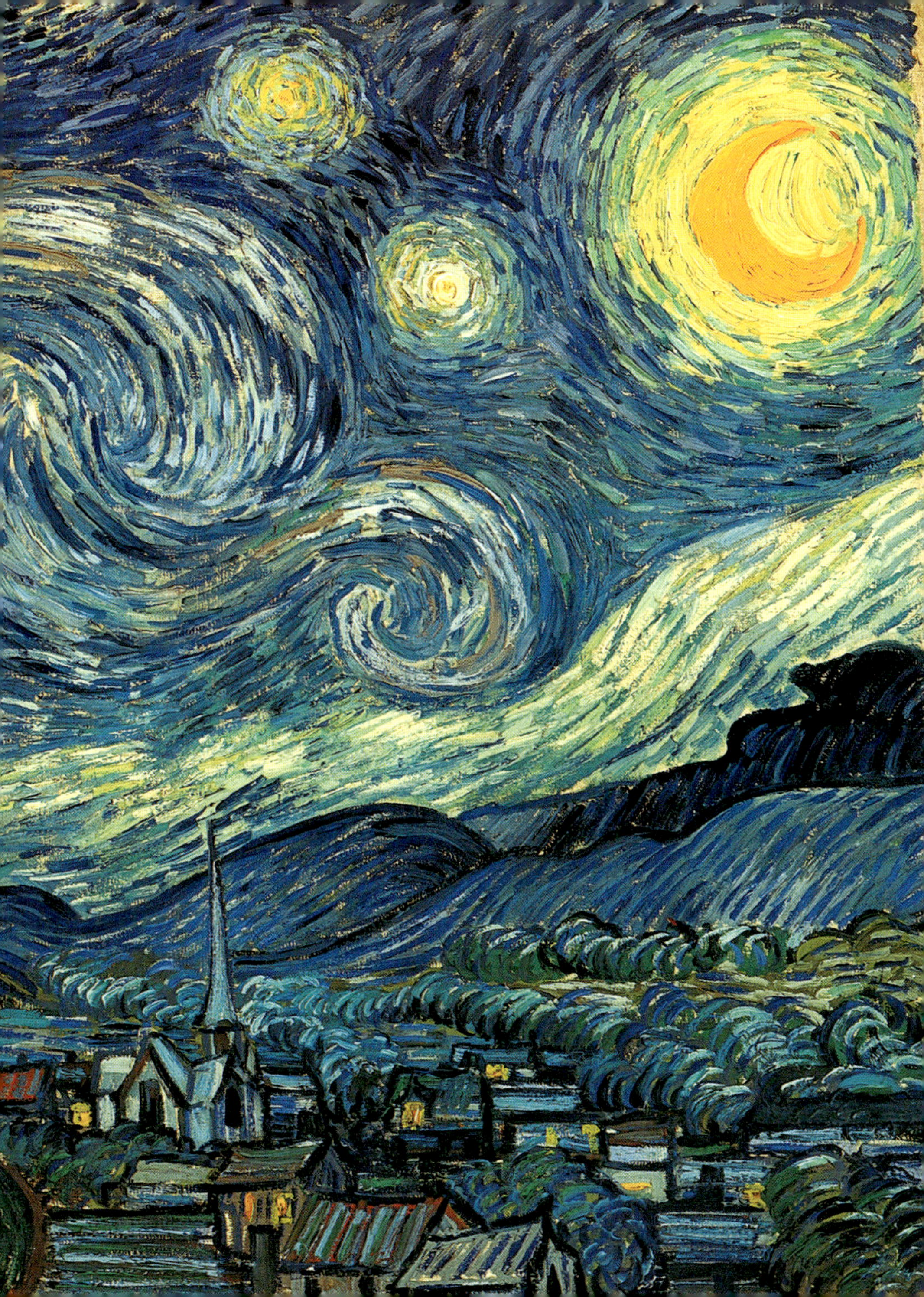

Back to the North

In the spring of 1890, after almost a year in the asylum at St-Rémy, Van Gogh's mental condition was not improving – he had recently suffered his most serious crisis to date, and his head was filled with overpowering memories of his life in the north. His dream of a Provençal artists' colony was long gone, and he devoted his time to a series of small paintings and drawings showing the Dutch peasants and thatched cottages he had first depicted almost a decade earlier. In May 1890 he yielded to his nostalgia and boarded a train to Paris. Dr Peyron completed the final report on his patient with a single word: "Cured." But this was simply a way of washing his hands of a troublesome case: he undoubtedly knew that Van Gogh was far from well.

In Paris Van Gogh had a happy reunion with Theo, who was now married and the proud father of a son named Vincent Willem. Theo's wife Jo recalled that when he showed his brother his infant namesake, both men had tears of joy in their eyes. But Jo and Theo were deeply worried about Van Gogh's mental state.

Auvers-sur-Oise

The happy reunion was simply a stop-over. Van Gogh spent just three days in Paris before continuing on to Auvers-sur-Oise, where Theo had arranged for his brother to live and paint under the care of Dr Paul Gachet. Gachet had treated other artists and was himself an amateur painter, and Theo hoped that he might be more successful than Dr Peyron in helping his brother.

Auvers had artistic connections that undoubtedly appealed to Van Gogh. Daubigny had settled there in 1861, and Pissarro, Cézanne, and Gauguin had all spent time in nearby Pontoise. On May 20, 1890 Van Gogh took the short train ride from Paris to Auvers. From the station he walked up the hill past the former house of Daubigny to Gachet's surgery. It was to be the last journey he ever took, but in Auvers he would also create some of his most moving paintings.

Portrait of Dr Gachet

Van Gogh felt an immediate kinship with the red-headed Gachet, writing to his sister Willemien on June 5, 1890 that the doctor was "a ready-made friend and something like a new brother would be – so much do we resemble each other physically, and morally too. He's very nervous and very bizarre himself." But Van Gogh also realized within a few days of his arrival that the doctor's fragile mental state meant he would not be of much help as a physician. He immediately warned Theo and Jo in a letter on May 24 that "we must IN NO WAY count on Dr. Gachet ... he's iller than I am.... When one blind man leads another blind man, do they not both fall into the ditch?"

In the portrait of his physician Van Gogh shows Dr. Gachet with an expression of profound melancholy, suggested by the greenish tinge to his face and the agitated turquoise dashes that swirl around him. On the table are two popular novels by the Goncourt brothers. The themes of these books – neurosis in *Germinie Lacerteux*, and the Paris art world in *Manette Salomon* – refer to the doctor's twin interests. The portrait is less a document of Dr Gachet's physical appearance than an expressive picture of his whole being. As Van Gogh explained in his letter to Willemien, "I don't try to do us by photographic resemblance but by our passionate expressions."

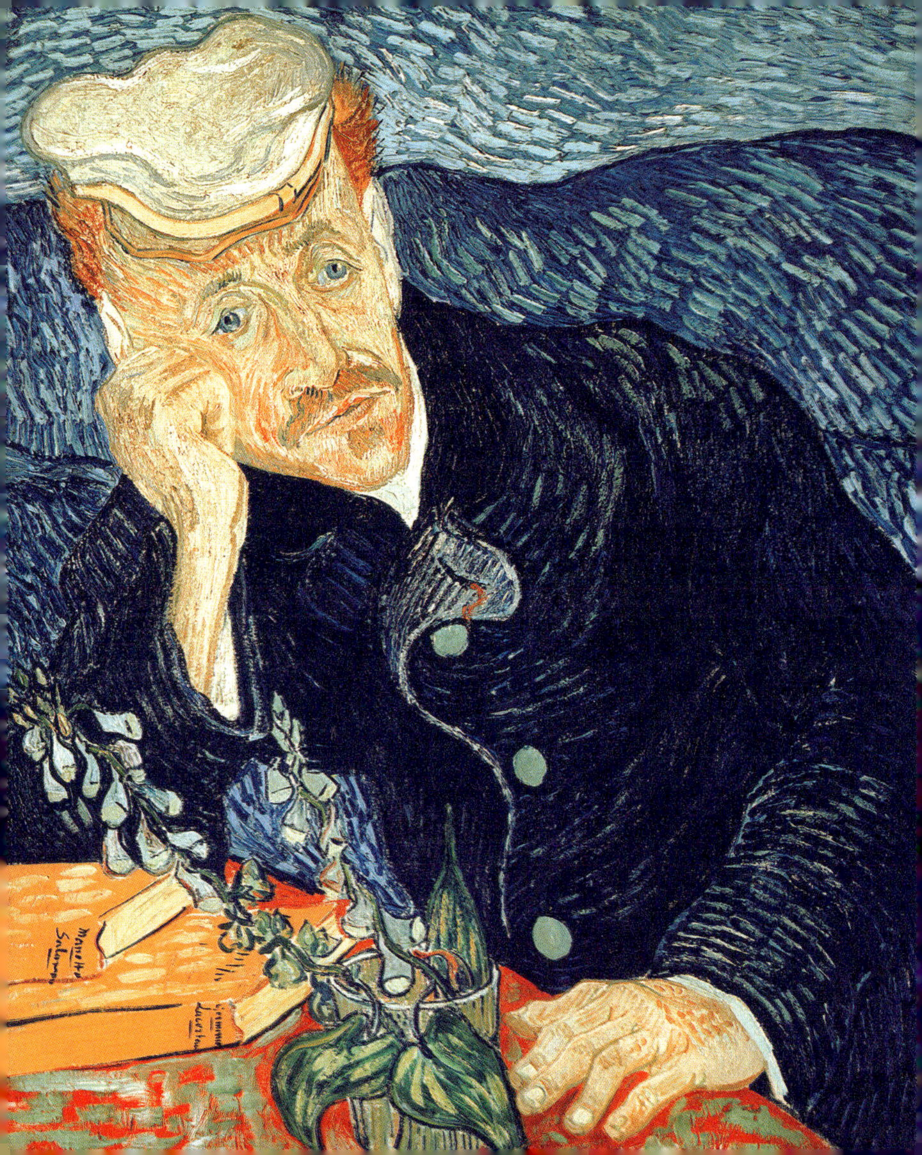
Manette Salomon

The Church in Auvers-sur-Oise
Vincent van Gogh, 1890

The Church in Auvers-sur-Oise

Despite his lack of faith in Dr Gachet's ability to treat him, Van Gogh was relatively content during his first few weeks in Auvers. He found cheap lodgings in a small café next to the town hall, and though his room was cramped, the friendly proprietors – Monsieur and Madame Ravoux – let him use a downstairs room as a studio when bad weather kept him indoors. Whenever possible, though, he much preferred to work outdoors. And he was delighted to be able to wander freely after the year of confinement in St-Rémy. Furthermore, the peasants and thatched cottages of Auvers reminded him of home.

The Church in Auvers-sur-Oise shows the small thirteenth-century church a few hundred yards along the narrow road from Van Gogh's lodgings. The image accurately portrays certain details of the church's Gothic architecture but the colours have been simplified and intensified, with the saturated blue of the sky standing in stark contrast to the orange and violet pigment thickly applied to the roof. The expressive power of the image is heightened by the way in which the building seems to writhe and flex as though animated by a mysterious force.

The intensity of Van Gogh's response to the church is explained in part by the fact that it reminded him of happier times. In his June 5 letter to Willemien he mentioned that the painting was "almost the same thing as the studies I did in Nuenen of the old tower and the cemetery." But if the building reminded him of home, he still felt ill at ease. Above the church the sky is threateningly dark, and the single figure – a local peasant woman – turns her back on us. Even in Auvers, Van Gogh sensed keenly his separation from those around him.

A Final Crisis

Van Gogh's relative calm did not last long. On June 30, 1890, Theo wrote to say that his son Vincent had been critically ill. Although the infant was out of danger, Van Gogh was deeply distressed nonetheless – perhaps remembering an earlier Vincent Willem, his older brother who had died as an infant. Van Gogh was then thrown into even deeper despair when Theo insisted on taking his new family to see their mother in Holland rather than spending the summer with him.

Wheat Field with Crows

Increasingly confused and melancholy, Van Gogh took to working in isolation outside Auvers, where he created a series of paintings of the empty fields above the town. He described the images in one of his last letters to Theo on July 10: "They're immense stretches of wheatfields under turbulent skies, and I made a point of trying to express sadness, extreme loneliness." The most powerful of these images, *Wheat Field with Crows*, appears almost to be a last testament. The threateningly dark sky, the ominous crows that circle overhead, and the path that reaches a dead end amidst the ripening corn, all seem to foretell the artist's approaching death.

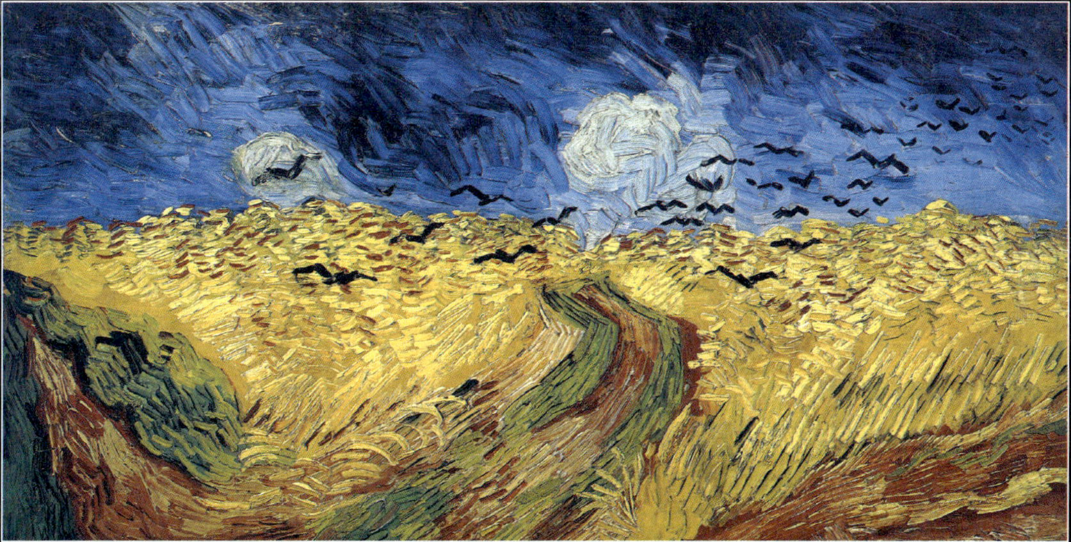

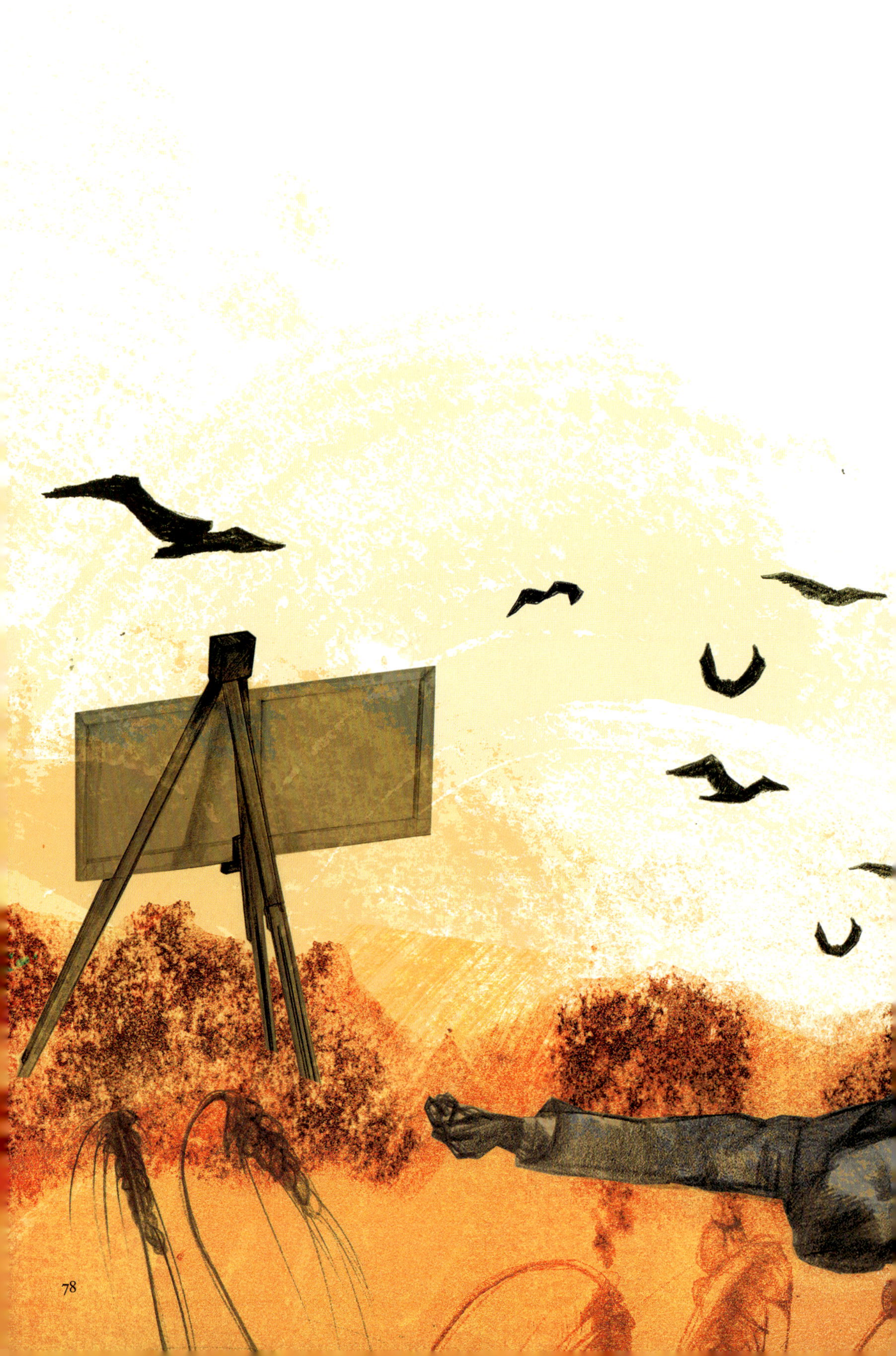

The End

On July 27, 1890, Van Gogh took his lunch as usual at the café where he lodged. He ate rather more quickly than normal then walked to one of his favourite painting spots above the town. What happened next will never be known for certain. Perhaps he continued to paint for a while. But at some point he put down his brush and picked up a revolver that he had stolen from a young acquaintance who used to hunt in the fields around Auvers. Taking aim at his own chest, he pulled the trigger.

The shot knocked him down but did not kill him. He staggered back to the café where his landlord summoned the local general practitioner, a Dr Mazery, who was soon joined by Dr Gachet. Together the two physicians examined the artist. They were relieved that the bullet had not struck the artist's heart, but as it was lodged deep within his chest, surgery to remove it was impossible.

Summoned by Dr Gachet, Theo arrived in all haste at noon the following day. At first he thought his brother might survive, but as the day passed, infection set in and Van Gogh's condition quickly deteriorated. As the end approached, Theo lay on the bed beside his brother, cradling his head in his arms. In the small hours of the next morning Van Gogh died.

Life After Death

Van Gogh died just as his reputation was beginning to grow. In early 1890, just a few months before his suicide, several of his paintings were displayed at exhibitions of modern art in Paris and Brussels. A number of important artists, amongst them Toulouse-Lautrec, Signac, and Monet, spoke highly of the works, and the influential art critic Albert Aurier called him a genius in the respected Parisian journal *Mercure de France*. But this recognition arrived too late. Van Gogh famously sold only one painting during his life, despite all of Theo's loyal efforts to find buyers. And Theo himself would not live to see his brother's posthumous success, following him into the grave just six months later. But by the mid-1890s Van Gogh was recognized as one of the greatest European painters.

Self-Portrait Dedicated to Paul Gauguin

In a second letter from Auvers to his sister Willemien on June 13, 1890, Van Gogh wrote that he wanted to make portraits that would go on being looked at for a century or more. With the profoundly expressive self-portraits that he painted in Arles he had already achieved this aim, though tragically he was not to know it. The graphic power of the intensely simplified draughtsmanship and colour, and the piercing nature of his haunted expression, continue to move viewers to this day. Equally affecting is the barely legible dedication to "my friend Paul Gauguin" that runs across the top of the painting, a reminder of a friendship that, like so much in Van Gogh's life, ended in sadness. Van Gogh's powerful emotions always made it hard for him to communicate with those around him. But his genius for conveying those emotions in visual form means that his art continues to speak to us more than a century after his death.

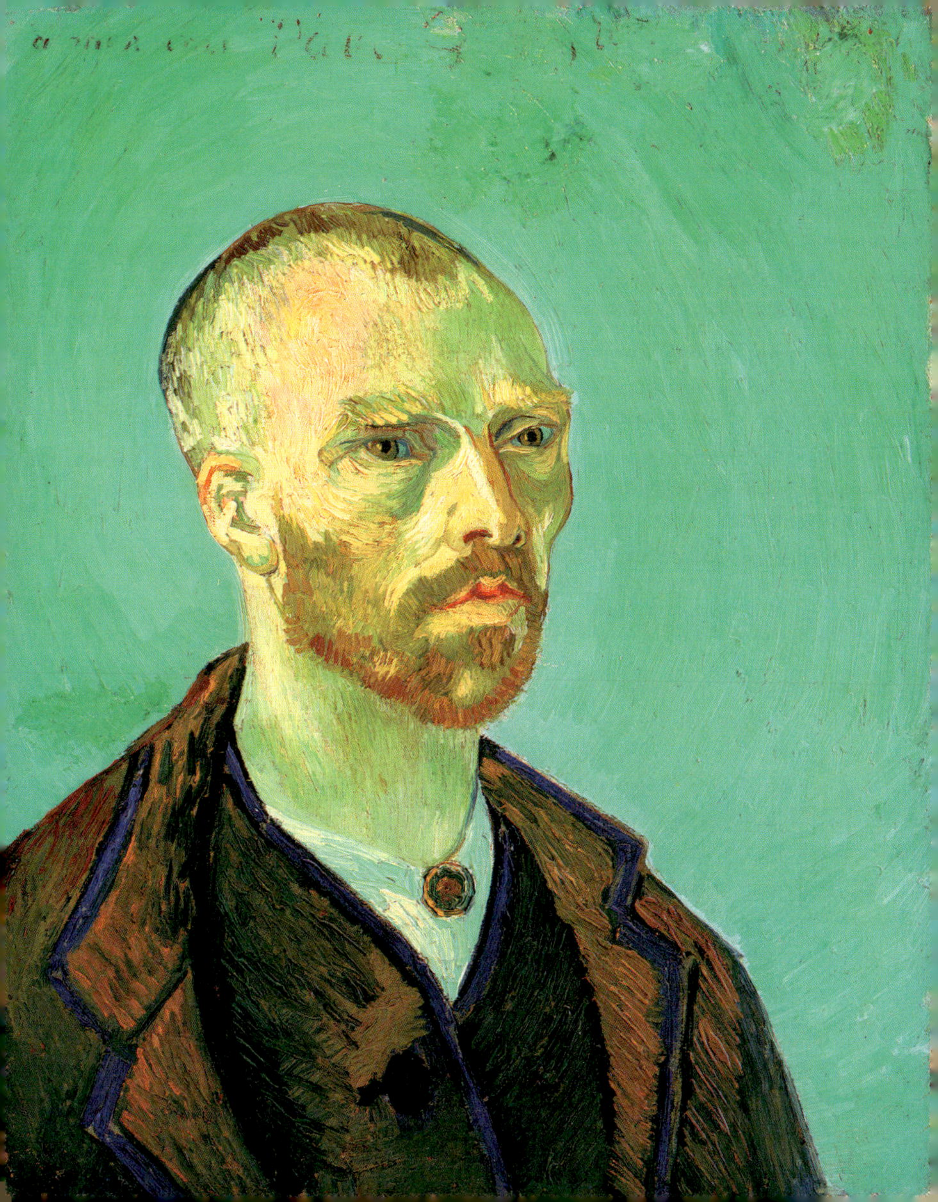

Glossary

ALIENATE To make unfriendly, hostile, or indifferent especially where attachment formerly existed; to cause (someone) to feel that she or he no longer belongs in a particular group, society, etc.

ASYLUM An institution for the care of the destitute or sick and especially the insane; a place of retreat and security.

AVANT-GARDE A group of people who develop new and often very surprising ideas in art, literature, etc.

BARBIZON SCHOOL Of, relating to, or being a school of mid-19th century French landscape painters whose naturalistic canvases were based on direct observation of nature.

DOCTRINE A set of ideas or beliefs that are taught or believed to be true; a principle or position or the body of principles in a branch of knowledge or system of belief; dogma.

ECSTASY A state of overwhelming emotion; rapturous delight.

IMPRESSIONISM A theory or practice in painting especially among French painters of about 1870 of depicting the natural appearances of objects by means of dabs or strokes of primary unmixed colors in order to simulate actual reflected light; the depiction (as in literature) of scene, emotion, or character by details intended to achieve a vividness or effectiveness more by evoking subjective and sensory impressions than by recreating an objective reality.

INERADICABLE Impossible to remove or forget.

LUCID Having full use of one's faculties; sane; clear to the understanding; intelligible.

LUMINOUS Emitting or reflecting usually steady, suffused, or glowing light; of or relating to light or to luminous flux; bathed in or exposed to steady light; shining.

MISSIVE A letter or other written message.

PIOUS Deeply religious : devoted to a particular religion.

POST-IMPRESSIONISM A theory or practice of art originating in France in the last quarter of the 19th century that in revolt against impressionism stresses variously volume, picture structure, or expressionism.

REDEMPTION The act of making something better or more acceptable; the act of saving people from sin and evil; the fact of being saved from sin or evil.

THEOLOGY The study of religious faith, practice, and experience; the study of God and God's relation to the world; a system of religious beliefs or ideas.

UNREQUITED Not shared or returned by someone else; not reciprocated or returned in kind.

UTOPIA A place of ideal perfection especially in laws, government, and social conditions; an impractical scheme for social improvement.

For More Information

Art Institute of Chicago

111 South Michigan Avenue

Chicago, IL 60603-6404

Website: http://www.artic.edu

The Art Institute of Chicago collects, preserves, and interprets works of art of the highest quality, representing the world's diverse artistic traditions, for the inspiration and education of the public and in accordance with the profession's highest ethical standards and practices.

The Getty

1200 Getty Center Drive

Los Angeles, CA 90049-1679

(310) 440-7300

Website: http://www.getty.edu

The J. Paul Getty Trust is a cultural and philanthropic institution dedicated to the presentation, conservation, and interpretation of the world's artistic legacy. The Getty is dedicated to the proposition that works of art are windows onto the world's diverse and intertwined histories, mirrors of humanity's innate imagination and creativity, and inspiration to envision the future.

The Metropolitan Museum of Art

1000 Fifth Avenue

New York, NY 10028

(212) 535-7710

Website: http://www.metmuseum.org

The Metropolitan Museum of Art collects, studies, conserves, and presents significant works of art across all times and cultures in order to connect people to creativity, knowledge, and ideas. The Met presents over 5,000 years of art from around the world for everyone to experience and enjoy. The Museum lives in three iconic sites in New York City—The Met Fifth Avenue, The Met Breuer, and The Met Cloisters. Millions of people also take part in The Met experience online.

The Museum of Modern Art (MoMA)
11 West 53rd Street
New York, NY 10019
(212) 708-9400
Website: https://www.moma.org

Founded in 1929 as an educational institution, The Museum of Modern Art is dedicated to being the foremost museum of modern art in the world. Through the leadership of its Trustees and staff, The Museum of Modern Art manifests this commitment by establishing, preserving, and documenting a permanent collection of the highest order that reflects the vitality, complexity and unfolding patterns of modern and contemporary art and by presenting exhibitions and educational programs of unparalleled significance. Central to The Museum of Modern Art's mission is the encouragement of an ever-deeper understanding and enjoyment of modern and contemporary art by the diverse local, national, and international audiences that it serves.

Van Gogh Museum (VGM)
Museumplein 6
P.O. Box 75366
1070 AJ Amsterdam
Tel.: +31 (0)20 570 5200
Website: https://www.vangoghmuseum.nl/en

The Van Gogh Museum makes the life and work of Vincent van Gogh and the art of his time accessible to as many people as possible in order to enrich and inspire them. The VGM is one of the leading museums in the world. The main objective of the VGM is the management and conservation of the collection and making this accessible to as many people as possible.

Websites

Because of the changing nature of internet links, Rosen Publishing has developed an online list of websites related to the subject of this book. This site is updated regularly. Please use this link to access this list:

http://www.rosenlinks.com/LGA/vangogh

For Further Reading

Bailey, Martin. *The Sunflowers Are Mine: The Story of van Gogh's Masterpiece.* London, UK: Frances Lincoln, 2013.

Bakker, Nienke, et al. *On the Verge of Insanity: Van Gogh and His Illness.* Brussels, Belgium: Mercatorfonds, 2016.

Bell, Julian. *Van Gogh: A Power Seething.* New York, NY: New Harvest, 2015.

Gayford, Martin. *The Yellow House: Van Gogh, Gauguin, and Nine Turbulent Weeks in Provence.* New York, NY: Mariner Books, 2008.

Groom, Gloria, et al. *Van Gogh's Bedrooms.* Chicago, IL: Art Institute of Chicago, 2016.

Kendall, Richard, et al. *Van Gogh and Nature.* Williamstown, MA: Clark Art Institute, 2015.

Metzger, Rainer, and Ingo F. Walther. *Van Gogh: Complete Works.* Cologne, Germany: Taschen, 2012.

Murphy, Bernadette. *Van Gogh's Ear.* New York, NY: Farrar, Straus and Giroux, 2016.

Naifeh, Steven, and Gregory White Smith. *Van Gogh: The Life.* New York, NY: Random House, 2012.

van Gogh, Vincent, and Ronald de Leeuw, ed. *The Letters of Vincent van Gogh.* New York, NY: Penguin, 1998.

van Gogh, Vincent, and H. Anna Suh, ed. *Van Gogh's Letters: The Mind of the Artist in Paintings, Drawings, and Words, 1875-1890.* New York, NY: Black Dog & Leventhal, 2010.

Walther, Ingo F. *Van Gogh.* Cologne, Germany: Taschen, 2016.

Bibliography

Ives, Colta, Susan Alyson Stein, Sjraar van Heugten and Marije Vellekoop. *Vincent van Gogh: The Drawings.* New York, NY: Metropolitan Museum of Art. 2005. Exhibition catalogue.

Jansen, Leo, Hans Luijten and Nienke Bakker, eds. *Vincent van Gogh—The Letters.* Amsterdam and The Hague, Netherlands: Van Gogh Museum and Huygens ING, 2009. Version: October 2013. http://vangoghletters.org. Scans of all Van Gogh's letters with translations, explanatory notes, etc.

Pickvance, Ronald. *Van Gogh in Arles.* New York, NY: Metropolitan Museum of Art, 1984. Exhibition catalogue.

Standring, Timothy J., and Louis van Tilborgh, eds. *Becoming Van Gogh.* Denver, CO: Denver Art Museum, 2012. Exhibition catalogue.

Sweetman, David. *The Love of Many Things: A Life of Vincent van Gogh.* London, UK: Hodder and Stoughton, 1990.

Vellekoop, Marije, and Nienke Bakker. *Van Gogh at Work.* New Haven, CT: Yale University Press, 2013.

Walther, Ingo F., *Vincent van Gogh, 1853–1890: Vision and Reality.* Cologne, Germany: Taschen, 2012.

Zemel, Carol M. *Van Gogh's Progress: Utopia, Modernity, and Late Nineteenth Century Art.* Berkeley, CA: University of California Press, 1997.

Index

A

absinthe, 26, 37, 40, 45
Académie Royale des Beaux-Arts, 16
Antwerp, Holland, 26, 27, 28, 32
Arles, France, 40–42, 45–47, 51, 52, 54, 57, 62, 63, 66, 80
Auvers-sur-Oise, France, 71, 75

B

Barbizon School, 16, 24, 25, 57, 66
Bearers of the Burden, The, 14
Bedroom, The, 42
Bernard, Émile, 34, 40, 57, 66
Borinage, Belgium, 12–13, 14, 16
Breton, Jules, 16, 25, 26
Bridges across the Seine at Asnières, 38

C

Café Table with Absinthe, 37
Church in Auvers-sur-Oise, The, 75
Cormon, Fernand, 34

D

Dutch Reformed Church, 8, 11, 16

G

Gachet, Paul, 71, 72, 75, 79
Gauguin, Paul, 34, 38, 58, 61, 71, 80
Ginoux, Joseph, 51
Goupil & Cie art gallery, 10, 11, 16, 21
Groot Zundert, Holland, 8

H

Hague School, The, 16
Harvest, The, 54, 57
Hoornik, Clasina ("Sien"), 17, 18, 24

I

Impressionism, 10, 31, 34

K

Koning, Arnold, 46

L

Livens, Horace, 27
London, England, 10, 11, 17, 18, 37
Loyer, Eugénie, 11, 17, 37

M

Mauve, Anton, 18, 32, 34
Michel, George, 21
Michelet, Jules, 18
Millet, Jean-François, 57, 63, 66
Miners' Wives Carrying Sacks, 14
Montmartre, 27, 31, 34, 35, 38
Montmartre: Windmills and Allotments, 31

N

Neo-Impressionism, 38
Night Café, The, 51, 54
Nuenen, Holland, 24, 26, 75

P

Paris, France, 10, 11, 21, 26, 32, 34, 40, 41, 47, 57, 61, 64, 70, 71, 72, 80
Peyron, Théophile, 62, 63, 70, 71
Plum Estate, Kameido, 32, 57
Portrait of Dr Gachet, 72
Post-Impressionism, 34, 38
Postman Joseph Roulin, 45
Potato Eaters, The, 24–25, 31, 57

R

Rain, 64
Roulin, Joseph, 45, 46

S

Self-Portrait Dedicated to Paul Gauguin, 80
Signac, Paul, 38, 40, 62, 80
Sorrow, 18
Sower with Setting Sun, 57
Starry Night, The, 66
St-Rémy, asylum at, 62, 63, 64, 66, 70, 75
Sunflowers, 58

T

Toulouse-Lautrec, Henri de, 34, 35, 80

V

van Gogh, Anna (mother), 8
van Gogh, Theo (brother), 7, 8, 9, 16, 17, 18, 21, 24–25, 26, 27, 28, 31, 37, 40, 42, 45, 46, 47, 51, 52, 53, 54, 58, 63, 64, 66, 70, 71, 76, 79, 80
van Gogh, Theodorus (father), 8, 9, 11, 16, 24, 26
van Gogh, Vincent
   in art school, 16
   in the asylum, 62–66
   childhood, 8–9
   death, 79
   doomed loves, 11, 17–18,
   early career, 10–11
   influence of Japanese art on, 32
   interest in color theory, 25
   interest in depicting peasants and poverty, 14, 17, 18, 24–25, 28
   legacy, 80
   letters by, 7, 9, 14, 17, 18, 21, 24–25, 37, 46, 47, 51, 52, 57, 58, 64, 66, 72, 75, 76, 80
   mental instability, 37, 47, 61, 62, 70, 76
   painting process, 37
   studies/career in theology, 11–12
   uncles, 8, 10, 11, 16
van Gogh, Willemien (sister), 8, 9, 72, 75, 80
Vos-Stricker, Kee, 17

W

Wheat Field with Crows, 76